PENGUIN BOOKS

FAIRY TALES FROM MANY LANDS

Born in London in 1867, Arthur Rackham was one of twelve children of a civil servant in the Admiralty Court. As a child he showed a precocious talent for drawing; and when, at seventeen, he became a clerk in the Westminster Fire Office, he also began part-time studies at the Lambeth School of Art. His first published drawing appeared in 1884, and in 1892 he gave up his clerkship to devote himself entirely to art, working for several years on the staff of the *Westminster Budget* but turning more and more to book illustration. In 1903 he married the artist Edythe Starkie, and soon thereafter, through his illustrations of *Sleeping Beauty, Cinderella,* and many other books, he achieved the great renown that his work still enjoys. He died in 1939.

·FAIRY TALES·
FROM MANY LANDS

·ILLUSTRATED·BY·
·ARTHUR·RACKHAM·

PENGUIN BOOKS

Penguin Books Ltd, Harmondsworth,
Middlesex, England
Penguin Books, 625 Madison Avenue,
New York, New York 10022, U.S.A.
Penguin Books Australia Ltd, Ringwood,
Victoria, Australia
Penguin Books Canada Limited, 2801 John Street,
Markham, Ontario, Canada L3R 1B4
Penguin Books (N.Z.) Ltd, 182–190 Wairau Road,
Auckland 10, New Zealand

First published under the title *The Allies' Fairy Book,* with
an Introduction by Edmund Gosse, 1916
This edition first published in the United States of America by
The Viking Press 1974
Published in Penguin Books 1978

LIBRARY OF CONGRESS CATALOGING IN PUBLICATION DATA
Main entry under title:
Fairy tales from many lands.
First ed. published in 1916 under title: The Allies' fairy book.
SUMMARY: Thirteen fairy tales from a variety of countries
including Japan, Yugoslavia, Portugal, and Belgium.
1. Fairy tales. [1. Fairy tales] I. Rackham, Arthur, 1867–1939.
PZ8.F16867   1978   398.2   78–16789
ISBN 0 14 00.4914 2

Printed in the United States of America by
The Book Press, Brattleboro, Vermont
Color printed by A. Hoen & Co., Inc., Baltimore, Maryland
Set in Caslon

"Jack the Giant-killer" is reprinted from *English Fairy Tales,* collected by Joseph Jacobs, published by David Nutt. "The Battle of the Birds" is reprinted from J. F. Campbell's *Popular Tales of the West Highlands.* "Lludd and Llevelys" is reprinted from Lady Charlotte Guest's version of the *Mabinogion.* "Guleesh" is reprinted from Dr. Douglas Hyde's *Beside the Fire.* "The Sleeping Beauty" is translated from the French of Charles Perrault by S. R. Littlewood. "Cesarino and the Dragon" is reprinted from Vol. II of G. W. Waters's *The Nights of Straparola,* published by Sidgwick & Jackson. "What Came of Picking Flowers" is reprinted from A. Lang's *Grey Fairy Book.* The three Japanese stories are from Lord Redesdale's *Tales of Old Japan.* "Frost" is reprinted from Ralston's *Russian Folk-Tales.* "The Golden Apple-Tree and the Nine Peahens" is reprinted from *Serbian Folk-Lore,* selected and translated by Madame Mijatovics. "The Last Adventure of Thyl Ulenspiegel" has been translated for the present volume from the romance of Charles de Coster.

CONTENTS

JACK THE GIANT-KILLER

WHEN good King Arthur reigned, there lived *English* near the Land's End of England, in the county of Cornwall, a farmer who had only one son, called Jack. He was brisk and of a ready lively wit, so that nobody or nothing could worst him.

In those days the Mount of Cornwall was kept by a huge giant named Cormoran. He was eighteen feet in height, and about three yards round the waist, of a fierce and grim countenance, the terror of all the neighbouring towns and villages. He lived in a cave in the midst of the Mount, and whenever he wanted food he would wade over to the mainland, where he would furnish himself with whatever came in his way. Everybody at his approach ran out of their houses, while he seized on their cattle, making nothing of carrying half a dozen oxen on his back at a time; and as for their sheep and hogs,

1

English he would tie them round his waist like a bunch of tallow-dips. He had done this for many years, so that all Cornwall was in despair.

One day Jack happened to be at the Town Hall when the magistrates were sitting in council about the Giant. He asked: "What reward will be given to the man who kills Cormoran?" "The giant's treasure," they said, "will be the reward." Quoth Jack: "Then let me undertake it."

So he got a horn, shovel, and pickaxe, and went over to the Mount in the beginning of a dark winter's evening, when he fell to work, and before morning had dug a pit twenty-two feet deep, and nearly as broad, covering it over with long sticks and straw. Then he strewed a little mould over it, so that it appeared like plain ground. Jack then placed himself on the opposite side of the pit, farthest from the giant's lodging, and, just at the break of day, he put the horn to his mouth and blew, Tantivy, Tantivy. This noise roused the giant, who rushed from his cave crying: "You incorrigible villain, are you come here to disturb my rest? You shall pay dearly for this. Satisfaction I will have, and this it shall be: I will take you whole and broil you for breakfast." He had no sooner uttered this than he tumbled into the pit and made the very foundations of the Mount to shake. "Oh, Giant," quoth Jack, "where are you now? Oh, faith, you are gotten now into Lob's Pound, where I will surely plague you for your threatening words: what do you think now of broiling me for your breakfast? Will no other diet serve you but poor Jack?" Then, having tantalized the giant for a while, he gave him a most weighty knock with his pickaxe on the very crown of his head and killed him on the spot.

Jack then filled up the pit with earth, and went to

2

JACK THE GIANT-KILLER

English

HE TUMBLED INTO THE PIT AND MADE THE VERY
FOUNDATIONS OF THE MOUNT TO SHAKE

search the cave, which he found contained much treasure.
When the magistrates heard of this they made a declaration he should henceforth be termed

Jack the Giant-killer

and presented him with a sword and a belt, on which were
written these words, embroidered in letters of gold :

> Here's the right valiant Cornish man
> Who slew the giant Cormoran

The news of Jack's victory soon spread over all the
West of England, so that another giant, named Blunderbore, hearing of it, vowed to be revenged on Jack if
ever he should light on him. This giant was the lord
of an enchanted castle situated in the midst of a lonesome

3

English wood. Now Jack, about four months afterwards, walking near this wood in his journey to Wales, being weary, seated himself near a pleasant fountain and fell fast asleep. While he was sleeping, the giant, coming there for water, discovered him, and knew him to be the far-famed Jack the Giant-killer by the lines written on his belt. Without ado, he took Jack on his shoulders and carried him towards his castle. Now, as they passed through a thicket, the rustling of the boughs awakened Jack, who was strangely surprised to find himself in the clutches of the giant. His terror was only begun, for, on entering the castle, he saw the ground strewed with human bones, and the giant told him his own would ere long be among them. After this the giant locked poor Jack in an immense chamber, leaving him there while he went to fetch another giant, his brother, living in the same wood, who might share in the meal on Jack.

After waiting some time, Jack, on going to the window, beheld afar off the two giants coming towards the castle. "Now," quoth Jack to himself, "my death or my deliverance is at hand." Now there were strong cords in a corner of the room in which Jack was, and two of these he took, and made a firm noose at the end ; and while the giants were unlocking the iron gate of the castle he threw the ropes over each of their heads. Then he drew the other ends across a beam, and pulled with all his might, so that he throttled them. Then, when he saw they were black in the face, he slid down one of the ropes and, drawing his sword, slew them both. Then, taking the giant's keys and unlocking the rooms, he found three fair ladies tied by the hair of their heads, almost starved to death. "Sweet ladies," quoth Jack, "I have destroyed this monster and his brutish brother, and obtained your liberties." This said he presented

4

them with the keys, and so proceeded on his journey *English* to Wales.

Jack made the best of his way by travelling as fast as he could, but lost his road, and was benighted, and could find no habitation until, coming into a narrow valley, he found a large house, and in order to get shelter took courage to knock at the gate. But what was his surprise when there came forth a monstrous giant with two heads ; yet he did not appear so fiery as the others were, for he was a Welsh giant, and what he did was by private and secret malice under the false show of friend- ship. Jack, having told his condition to the giant, was shown into a bedroom, where, in the dead of night, he heard his host in another apartment muttering these words :

> "Though here you lodge with me this night,
> You shall not see the morning light :
> My club shall dash your brains outright ! "

" Say'st thou so ? " quoth Jack ; " that is like one of your Welsh tricks, yet I hope to be cunning enough for you." Then, getting out of bed, he laid a billet in the bed in his stead, and hid himself in a corner of the room. At the dead time of the night in came the Welsh giant, who struck several heavy blows on the bed with his club, thinking he had broken every bone in Jack's skin. The next morning Jack, laughing in his sleeve, gave him hearty thanks for his night's lodging. "How have you rested ? " quoth the giant ; " did you not feel anything in the night ? " " No," quoth Jack, " nothing but a rat, which gave me two or three slaps with her tail." With that, greatly wondering, the giant led Jack to breakfast, bringing him a bowl containing four gallons of hasty pudding. Being loath to let the giant think it too much for him, Jack put a large leather bag under his loose coat in such a way that he could convey the

5

English pudding into it without its being perceived. Then, telling the giant he would show him a trick, taking a knife, Jack ripped open the bag, and out came all the hasty pudding. Whereupon, saying, " Odds splutters hur nails, hur can do that trick hurself," the monster took the knife, and ripping open his own belly, fell down dead.

Now it happened in these days that King Arthur's only son asked his father to give him a large sum of money, in order that he might go and seek his fortune in the principality of Wales, where lived a beautiful lady possessed with seven evil spirits. The king did his best to persuade his son from it, but in vain ; so at last he gave way and the prince set out with two horses, one loaded with money, the other for himself to ride upon. Now after several days' travel he came to a market-town in Wales, where he beheld a vast crowd of people gathered together. The prince asked the reason of it, and was told that they had arrested a corpse for several large sums of money which the deceased owed when he died. The prince replied that it was a pity creditors should be so cruel, and said : " Go bury the dead, and let his creditors come to my lodging, and there their debts shall be paid." They came in such great numbers that before night he had only twopence left for himself.

Now Jack the Giant-killer, coming that way, was so taken with the generosity of the prince that he desired to be his servant. This being agreed upon, the next morning they set forward on their journey together, when, as they were riding out of the town, an old woman called after the prince, saying : " He has owed me twopence these seven years ; pray pay me as well as the rest." Putting his hand in his pocket, the prince gave the woman all he had left, so that after their day's food, which cost what small store Jack had by him, they were without a penny between them.

6

When the sun got low, the king's son said: "Jack, *English* since we have no money, where can we lodge this night?"

But Jack replied: "Master, we'll do well enough, for I have an uncle lives within two miles of this place; he is a huge and monstrous giant with three heads. He'll fight five hundred men in armour, and make them to fly before him."

"Alas!" quoth the prince, "what shall we do there? He'll certainly chop us up at a mouthful. Nay, we are scarce enough to fill one of his hollow teeth!"

"It is no matter for that," quoth Jack; "I myself will go before and prepare the way for you; therefore stop here and wait till I return." Jack then rode away at full speed, and coming to the gate of the castle, he knocked so loud that he made the neighbouring hills resound. The giant roared out at this like thunder: "Who's there?"

Jack answered: "None but your poor cousin Jack."

Quoth he: "What news with my poor cousin Jack?"

He replied: "Dear uncle, heavy news, God wot!"

"Prithee," quoth the giant, "what heavy news can come to me? I am a giant with three heads, and besides thou knowest I can fight five hundred men in armour, and make them fly like chaff before the wind."

"Oh, but," quoth Jack, "here's the king's son a-coming with a thousand men in armour to kill you and destroy all that you have!"

"Oh, cousin Jack," said the giant, "this is heavy news indeed! I will immediately run and hide myself, and thou shalt lock, bolt, and bar me in, and keep the keys until the prince is gone." Having secured the giant, Jack fetched his master, when they made themselves heartily merry whilst the poor giant lay trembling in a vault under the ground.

7

English Early in the morning Jack furnished his master with a fresh supply of gold and silver, and then sent him three miles forward on his journey, at which time the prince was pretty well out of the smell of the giant. Jack then returned, and let the giant out of the vault, who asked what he should give him for keeping the castle from destruction. "Why," quoth Jack, "I want nothing but the old coat and cap, together with the old rusty sword and slippers which are at your bed's head." Quoth the giant: "You know not what you ask; they are the most precious things I have. The coat will keep you invisible, the cap will tell you all you want to know, the sword cuts asunder whatever you strike, and the shoes are of extraordinary swiftness. But you have been very serviceable to me, therefore take them with all my heart." Jack thanked his uncle, and then went off with them. He soon overtook his master and they quickly arrived at the house of the lady the prince sought, who, finding the prince to be a suitor, prepared a splendid banquet for him. After the repast was concluded, she told him she had a task for him. She wiped his mouth with a handkerchief, saying: "You must show me that handkerchief to-morrow morning, or else you will lose your head." With that she put it in her bosom. The prince went to bed in great sorrow, but Jack's cap of knowledge informed him how it was to be obtained. In the middle of the night she called upon her familiar spirit to carry her to Lucifer. But Jack put on his coat of darkness and his shoes of swiftness, and was there as soon as she was. When she entered the place of the demon, she gave the handkerchief to him, and he laid it upon a shelf, whence Jack took it and brought it to his master, who showed it to the lady next day, and so saved his life. On that day she gave the prince a kiss and told him he must show her the lips

8

to-morrow morning that she kissed that night, or lose *English* his head.

"Ah!" he replied, "if you kiss none but mine, I will."

"That is neither here nor there," said she; "if you do not, death's your portion!"

At midnight she went as before, and was angry with the demon for letting the handkerchief go. "But now," quoth she, "I will be too hard for the king's son, for I will kiss thee, and he is to show me thy lips." Which she did, and Jack, when she was not standing by, cut off Lucifer's head and brought it under his invisible coat to his master, who the next morning pulled it out by the horns before the lady. This broke the enchantment and the evil spirit left her and she appeared in all her beauty. They were married the next morning and soon after went to the court of King Arthur, where Jack, for his many great exploits, was made one of the Knights of the Round Table.

Jack soon went searching for giants again, but he had not ridden far when he saw a cave, near the entrance of which he beheld a giant sitting upon a block of timber, with a knotted iron club by his side. His goggle eyes were like flames of fire, his countenance grim and ugly, and his cheeks like a couple of large flitches of bacon, while the bristles of his beard resembled rods of iron wire, and the locks that hung down upon his brawny shoulders were like curled snakes or hissing adders. Jack alighted from his horse, and, putting on the coat of darkness, went up close to the giant, and said softly: "Oh! are you there? It will not be long before I take you fast by the beard." The giant all this while could not see him, on account of his invisible coat, so that Jack, coming up close to the monster, struck a blow with his sword at his head, but, missing his aim, he cut off

9

English the nose instead. At this the giant roared like claps of thunder, and began to lay about him with his iron club like one stark mad. But Jack, running behind, drove his sword up to the hilt in the giant's back, so that he fell down dead. This done, Jack cut off the giant's head, and sent it, with his brother's also, to King Arthur, by a wagoner he hired for that purpose.

Jack now resolved to enter the giant's cave in search of his treasure, and, passing along through a great many windings and turnings, he came at length to a large room paved with freestone, at the upper end of which was a boiling cauldron, and on the right hand a large table, at which the giant used to dine. Then he came to a window, barred with iron, through which he looked and beheld a vast number of miserable captives, who, seeing him, cried out: "Alas! young man, art thou come to be one amongst us in this miserable den?"

"Ay," quoth Jack, "but pray tell me what is the meaning of your captivity?"

"We are kept here," said one, "till such time as the giants have a wish to feast, and then the fattest among us is slaughtered! And many are the times they have dined upon murdered men!"

"Say you so?" quoth Jack, and straightway unlocked the gate and let them free, and they all rejoiced like condemned men at sight of a pardon. Then searching the giant's coffers, he shared the gold and silver equally amongst them and took them to a neighbouring castle, where they all feasted and made merry over their deliverance.

But in the midst of all this mirth a messenger brought news that one Thunderell, a giant with two heads, having heard of the death of his kinsmen, had come from the northern dales to be revenged on Jack, and was within a mile of the castle, the country people flying

10

At the dead time of the night in came the
Welsh giant

*In a twinkling the giant put each garden,
and orchard, and castle in the bundle as
they were before*

before him like chaff. But Jack was not a bit daunted *English* and said : " Let him come ! I have a tool to pick his teeth ; and you, ladies and gentlemen, walk out into the garden, and you shall witness this giant Thunderell's death and destruction."

The castle was situated in the midst of a small island surrounded by a moat thirty feet deep and twenty feet wide, over which lay a drawbridge. So Jack employed men to cut through this bridge on both sides, nearly to the middle ; and then, dressing himself in his invisible coat, he marched against the giant with his sword of sharpness. Although the giant could not see Jack, he smelt his approach, and cried out in these words :

> " Fee, fi, fo, fum !
> I smell the blood of an Englishman !
> Be he alive or be he dead,
> I'll grind his bones to make me bread ! "

" Say'st thou so ? " said Jack ; " then thou art a monstrous miller indeed." The giant cried out again : " Art thou that villain who killed my kinsmen ? Then I will tear thee with my teeth, suck thy blood, and grind thy bones to powder."

" You'll have to catch me first," quoth Jack, and throwing off his invisible coat, so that the giant might see him, and putting on his shoes of swiftness, he ran from the giant, who followed like a walking castle, so that the very foundations of the earth seemed to shake at every step. Jack led him a long dance, in order that the gentlemen and ladies might see ; and at last, to end the matter, ran lightly over the drawbridge, the giant, in full speed, pursuing him with his club. Then, coming to the middle of the bridge, the giant's great weight broke it down, and he tumbled headlong into the water, where he rolled and wallowed like a whale.

11

English Jack, standing by the moat, laughed at him all the while ; but though the giant foamed to hear him scoff, and plunged from place to place in the moat, yet he could not get out to be revenged. Jack at length got a cart-rope and cast it over the two heads of the giant, and drew him ashore by a team of horses, and then cut off both his heads with his sword of sharpness and sent them to King Arthur.

After some time spent in mirth and pastime, Jack, taking leave of the knights and ladies, set out for new adventures. Through many woods he passed, and came at length to the foot of a high mountain. Here, late at night, he found a lonesome house, and knocked at the door, which was opened by an aged man with a head as white as snow. " Father," said Jack, " can you lodge a benighted traveller that has lost his way ? " " Yes," said the old man ; " you are right welcome to my poor cottage." Whereupon Jack entered, and down they sat together, and the old man began to speak as follows : " Son, I see by your belt you are the great conqueror of giants, and behold, my son, on the top of this mountain is an enchanted castle ; this is kept by a giant named Galligantua, and he, by the help of an old conjurer, betrays many knights and ladies into his castle, where by magic art they are transformed into sundry shapes and forms. But above all, I grieve for a duke's daughter whom they fetched from her father's garden, carrying her through the air in a burning chariot drawn by fiery dragons, when they secured her within the castle, and transformed her into a white hind. And though many knights have tried to break the enchantment and work her deliverance, yet no one could accomplish it, on account of two dreadful griffins which are placed at the castle gate and which destroy every one who comes near. But you, my son, may pass by them undiscovered, where on

12

the gates of the castle you will find engraven in large *English* letters how the spell may be broken." Jack gave the old man his hand, and promised that in the morning he would venture his life to free the lady.

In the morning Jack arose and put on his invisible coat and magic cap and shoes, and prepared himself for the fray. Now when he had reached the top of the mountain he soon discovered the two fiery griffins, but passed them without fear, because of his invisible coat. When he had got beyond them, he found upon the gates of the castle a golden trumpet hung by a silver chain, under which these lines were engraved :

> Whoever shall this trumpet blow
> Shall soon the giant overthrow
> And break the black enchantment straight
> So all shall be in happy state

Jack had no sooner read this but he blew the trumpet, at which the castle trembled to its vast foundations, and the giant and conjurer were in horrid confusion, biting their thumbs and tearing their hair, knowing their wicked reign was at an end. Then the giant stooping to take up his club, Jack at one blow cut off his head ; whereupon the conjurer, mounting up into the air, was carried away in a whirlwind. Then the enchantment was broken, and all the lords and ladies who had so long been transformed into birds and beasts returned to their proper shapes, and the castle vanished away in a cloud of smoke. This being done, the head of Galligantua was likewise, in the usual manner, conveyed to the Court of King Arthur, where, the very next day, Jack followed, with the knights and ladies who had been delivered. Whereupon, as a reward for his good services, the king prevailed upon the duke to bestow his daughter in marriage on honest Jack. So married they were, and

13

English the whole kingdom was filled with joy at the wedding.
Furthermore, the king bestowed on Jack a noble castle,
with a very beautiful estate thereto belonging, where
he and his lady lived in great joy and happiness all the
rest of their days.

THE BATTLE OF THE BIRDS

THERE was once a time when every creature and bird *Scotch* was gathering to battle. The son of the King of Tethertown said that he would go to see the battle, and that he would bring sure word home to his father the king, who would be king of the creatures this year. The battle was over before he arrived, all but one fight, between a great black raven and a snake, and it seemed as if the snake would get the victory over the raven. When the king's son saw this, he helped the raven, and with one blow he takes the head off the snake. When the raven had taken breath, and saw that the snake was dead, he said: "For thy kindness to me this day I will give thee a sight. Come up now on the roof of my two wings." The king's son mounted upon the raven, and, before he stopped, he took him over seven Bens, and seven Glens, and seven Mountain Moors.

"Now," said the raven, "seest thou that house yonder? Go now to it. It is a sister of mine that makes her dwelling in it; and I will go bail that thou art welcome. And if she asks thee, Wert thou at the battle of the birds? say thou that thou wert. And if she asks, Didst thou see my likeness? say that thou sawest it. But be sure that thou meetest me

15

Scotch to-morrow morning here, in this place." The king's son got good and right good treatment this night. Meat of each meat, drink of each drink, warm water to his feet, and a soft bed for his limbs.

On the next day the raven gave him the same sight over seven Bens, and seven Glens, and seven Mountain Moors. They saw a bothy far off, but, though far off, they were soon there. He got good treatment this night, as before—plenty of meat and drink, and warm water to his feet, and a soft bed to his limbs—and on the next day it was the same thing.

On the third morning, instead of seeing the raven as at the other times, who should meet him but the handsomest lad he ever saw, with a bundle in his hand. The king's son asked this lad if he had seen a big black raven. Said the lad to him : " Thou wilt never see the raven again, for I am that raven. I was put under spells ; it was meeting thee that loosed me, and for that thou art getting this bundle. Now," said the lad, " thou wilt turn back on the self-same steps, and thou wilt lie a night in each house, as thou wert before ; but thy lot is not to loose the bundle which I gave thee till thou art in the place where thou wouldst most wish to dwell."

The king's son turned his back to the lad, and his face to his father's house ; and he got lodging from the raven's sisters, just as he got it when going forward. When he was nearing his father's house he was going through a close wood. It seemed to him that the bundle was growing heavy, and he thought he would look what was in it.

When he loosed the bundle, it was not without astonishing himself. In a twinkling he sees the very grandest place he ever saw. A great castle, and an orchard about the castle, in which was every kind of fruit and herb. He stood full of wonder and regret for having loosed the bundle—it was not

16

in his power to put it back again—and he would have wished *Scotch* this pretty place to be in the pretty little green hollow that was opposite his father's house ; but, at one glance, he sees a great giant coming towards him.

"Bad's the place where thou hast built thy house, king's son," says the giant. "Yes, but it is not here I would wish it to be, though it happened to be here by mishap," says the king's son. "What's the reward thou wouldst give me for putting it back in the bundle as it was before ? " "What's the reward thou wouldst ask ? " says the king's son. "If thou wilt give me the first son thou hast when he is seven years of age," says the giant. "Thou wilt get that if I have a son," said the king's son.

In a twinkling the giant put each garden, and orchard, and castle in the bundle as they were before. "Now," says the giant, "take thou thine own road, and I will take my road ; but mind thy promise, and though thou shouldst forget, I will remember."

The king's son took to the road, and at the end of a few days he reached the place he was fondest of. He loosed the bundle, and the same place was just as it was before. And when he opened the castle door he sees the handsomest maiden he ever cast eye upon. "Advance, king's son," said the pretty maid ; "everything is in order for thee, if thou wilt marry me this very night." "It's I am the man that is willing," said the king's son. And on the same night they married.

But at the end of a day and seven years, what great man is seen coming to the castle but the giant. The king's son, who had now succeeded his father, minded his promise to the giant, and till now he had not told his promise to the queen. "Leave thou the matter between me and the giant," says the queen.

"Turn out thy son," says the giant ; "mind your promise." "Thou wilt get that," says the king, "when his

17

Scotch mother puts him in order for his journey." The queen arrayed the cook's son, and she gave him to the giant by the hand. The giant went away with him ; but he had not gone far when he put a rod in the hand of the little laddie. The giant asked him : " If thy father had that rod, what would he do with it ? " " If my father had that rod he would beat the dogs and the cats, if they would be going near the king's meat," said the little laddie. " Thou'rt the cook's son," said the giant. He catches him by the two small ankles and knocks him—" Sgleog "—against the stone that was beside him. The giant turned back to the castle in rage and madness, and he said that if they did not turn out the king's son to him, the highest stone of the castle would be the lowest. Said the queen to the king : " We'll try it yet ; the butler's son is of the same age as our son." She arrayed the butler's son, and she gives him to the giant by the hand. The giant had not gone far when he put the rod in his hand. " If thy father had that rod," said the giant, " what would he do with it ? " " He would beat the dogs and cats when they would be coming near the king's bottles and glasses." " Thou art the son of the butler," says the giant, and dashed his brains out too. The giant returned in very great rage and anger. The earth shook under the soles of his feet, and the castle shook and all that was in it. " Out here thy son," says the giant, " or in a twinkling the stone that is highest in the dwelling will be the lowest." So needs must they had to give the king's son to the giant.

The giant took him to his own house, and he reared him as his own son. On a day of days when the giant was from home, the lad heard the sweetest music he ever heard in a room at the top of the giant's house. At a glance he saw the finest face he had ever seen. It was the giant's youngest daughter, who beckoned to him to come a bit nearer to her, and she told him to go this time, but to be sure to be at the same place about that dead midnight.

18

And as he promised he did. The giant's daughter was *Scotch* at his side in a twinkling, and she said : " To-morrow thou wilt get the choice of my two sisters to marry ; but say thou that thou wilt not take either, but me. My father wants me to marry the son of the King of the Green City, but I don't like him." On the morrow the giant took out his three daughters, and he said : " Now, son of the King of Tether-town, thou hast not lost by living with me so long. Thou wilt get to wife one of the two eldest of my daughters, and with her leave to go home with her the day after the wedding."

" If thou wilt give me this pretty little one," says the king's son, " I will take thee at thy word."

The giant's wrath kindled, and he said : " Before thou gett'st her thou must do the three things that I ask thee to do." " Say on," says the king's son. The giant took him to the byre. " Now," says the giant, " the dung of a hundred cattle is here, and it has not been cleansed for seven years. I am going from home to-day, and if this byre is not cleaned before night comes, so clean that a golden apple will run from end to end of it, not only thou shalt not get my daughter, but 'tis a drink of thy blood that will quench my thirst this night." He begins cleaning the byre, but it was just as well to keep baling the great ocean. After midday, when sweat was blinding him, the giant's young daughter came where he was, and she said to him : " Thou art being punished, king's son." " I am that," says the king's son. " Come over," says she, " and lay down thy weariness." " I will do that," says he, " there is but death awaiting me, at any rate." He sat down near her. He was so tired that he fell asleep beside her. When he awoke, the giant's daughter was not to be seen, but the byre was so well cleaned that a golden apple would run from end to end of it. In comes the giant, and he said : " Thou hast cleaned the byre, king's son ? " " I have cleaned it," says he. " Somebody

19

Scotch cleaned it," says the giant. " Thou didst not clean it, at all events," said the king's son. " Yes, yes," says the giant, " since thou wert so active to-day, thou wilt get to this time to-morrow to thatch this byre with birds' down—birds with no two feathers of one colour." The king's son was on foot before the sun ; he caught up his bow and his quiver of arrows to kill the birds. He took to the moors, but if he did, the birds were not so easy to take. He was running after them till the sweat was blinding him. About mid-day who should come but the giant's daughter. " Thou art exhausting thyself, king's son," says she. " I am," said he. " There fell but these two blackbirds, and both of one colour." " Come over and lay down thy weariness on this pretty hillock," says the giant's daughter. " It's I am willing," says he. He thought she would aid him this time too, and he sat down near her, and he was not long there till he fell asleep.

When he awoke, the giant's daughter was gone. He thought he would go back to the house, and he sees the byre thatched with the feathers. When the giant came home he said : " Thou hast thatched the byre, king's son ? " " I thatched it," says he. " Somebody thatched it," says the giant. " Thou didst not thatch it," says the king's son. " Yes, yes ! " says the giant. " Now," says the giant, " there is a fir-tree beside that loch down there, and there is a magpie's nest in its top. The eggs thou wilt find in the nest. I must have them for my first meal. Not one must be burst or broken, and there are five in the nest." Early in the morning the king's son went where the tree was, and that tree was not hard to hit upon. Its match was not in the whole wood. From the foot to the first branch was five hundred feet. The king's son was going all round the tree. She came who was always bringing help to him. " Thou art losing the skin of thy hands and feet." " Ach ! I am," says he. " I am no sooner up than down." " This

20

is no time for stopping," says the giant's daughter. She *Scotch*
thrust finger after finger into the tree, till she made a ladder
for the king's son to go up to the magpie's nest. When he
was at the nest, she said : " Make haste now with the eggs,
for my father's breath is burning my back." In her hurry
she left her little finger in the top of the tree. " Now," says
she, " thou wilt go home with the eggs quickly, and thou
wilt get me to marry to-night if thou canst know me. I
and my two sisters will be arrayed in the same garments,
and made like each other, but look at me when my father
says, ' Go to thy wife, king's son,' and thou wilt see a hand
without a little finger." He gave the eggs to the giant.
" Yes, yes ! " says the giant, " be making ready for thy
marriage."

Then indeed there was a wedding, and it " was " a wedding ! Giants and gentlemen, and the son of the King of
the Green City was in the midst of them. They were
married, and the dancing began, and that was a dance !
The giant's house was shaking from top to bottom. But
bedtime came, and the giant said : " It is time for thee to
go to rest, son of the King of Tethertown ; take thy bride
with thee from amidst those."

She put out the hand off which the little finger was, and
he caught her by the hand.

"Thou hast aimed well this time too ; but there is no
knowing but we may meet thee another way," said the
giant.

But to rest they went. " Now," says she, " sleep not, or
else thou diest. We must fly quick, quick, or for certain
my father will kill thee."

Out they went, and on the blue-grey filly in the stable
they mounted. " Stop a while," says she, " and I will play
a trick on the old hero." She jumped down, and cut an apple
into nine shares, and she put two shares at the head of the
bed, and two shares at the foot of the bed, and two shares

21

Scotch at the door of the kitchen, and two shares at the big door, and one outside the house.

The giant awoke and called : " Are you asleep ? " " We are not yet," said the apple that was at the head of the bed. At the end of a while he called again. " We are not yet," said the apple that was at the foot of the bed. A while after this he called again. " We are not yet," said the apple at the kitchen door. The giant called again. The apple that was at the big door answered. " You are now going far from me," says the giant. " We are not yet," says the apple that was outside the house. " You are flying," says the giant. The giant jumped on his feet, and to the bed he went, but it was cold—empty.

" My own daughter's tricks are trying me," said the giant. " Here's after them," says he.

In the mouth of day, the giant's daughter said that her father's breath was burning her back. " Put thy hand, quick," said she, " in the ear of the grey filly, and whatever thou findest in it, throw it behind thee." " There is a twig of sloe-tree," said he. " Throw it behind thee," said she.

No sooner did he that than there were twenty miles of blackthorn wood, so thick that scarce a weasel could go through it. The giant came headlong, and there he is fleecing his head and neck in the thorns.

" My own daughter's tricks are here as before," said the giant ; " but if I had my own big axe and wood-knife here, I would not be long making a way through this." He went home for the big axe and the wood-knife, and sure he was not long on his journey, and he was the boy behind the big axe. He was not long making a way through the blackthorn. " I will leave the axe and the wood-knife here till I return," says he. " If thou leave them," said a hoodie that was in a tree, " we will steal them."

" You will do that same," says the giant, " but I will set

22

them home." He returned and left them at the house. At Scotch
the heat of day the giant's daughter felt her father's breath
burning her back.

"Put thy finger in the filly's ear, and throw behind thee
whatever thou findest in it." He got a splinter of grey stone,
and in a twinkling there were twenty miles, by breadth and
height, of great grey rock behind them. The giant came
full pelt, but past the rock he could not go.

"The tricks of my own daughter are the hardest things
that ever met me," says the giant ; "but if I had my lever
and my mighty mattock, I would not be long making my
way through this rock also."

There was no help for it but to turn the chase for them ;
and he was the boy to split the stones. He was not long
making a road through the rock. "I will leave the tools
here, and I will return no more."

"If thou leave them," said the hoodie, "we will steal
them."

"Do that if thou wilt ; there is no time to go back." At
the time of breaking the watch, the giant's daughter said
that she was feeling her father's breath burning her back.
"Look in the filly's ear, king's son, or else we are lost."
He did so, and it was a bladder of water that was in her ear
this time. He threw it behind him, and there was a fresh-
water loch, twenty miles in length and breadth, behind
them.

The giant came on, but with the speed he had on him he
was in the middle of the loch, and he went under, and he
rose no more.

On the next day the young companions were come in
sight of his father's house. "Now," said she, "my father
is drowned, and he won't trouble us any more ; but before
we go any farther," says she, "go thou to thy father's house
and tell that thou hast the like of me ; but this is thy lot,
let neither man nor creature kiss thee, for if thou dost thou

Scotch wilt not remember that thou hast ever seen me." Every one he met was giving him welcome and luck, and he charged his father and mother not to kiss him; but as mishap was to be, an old greyhound was in and she knew him, and jumped up to his mouth, and after that he did not remember the giant's daughter.

She was sitting at the well's side as he left her, but the king's son was not coming. In the mouth of night she climbed up into a tree of oak that was beside the well, and she lay in the fork of the tree all that night. A shoemaker had a house near the well, and about midday on the morrow the shoemaker asked his wife to go for a drink for him out of the well. When the shoemaker's wife reached the well, and when she saw the shadow of her that was in the tree, thinking of it that it was her own shadow—and she never thought till now that she was so handsome—she gave a cast to the dish that was in her hand, and it was broken on the ground, and she took herself to the house without vessel or water.

"Where is the water, wife?" said the shoemaker. "Thou shambling, contemptible old carle, without grace, I have stayed too long thy water and wood thrall." "I am thinking, wife, that thou hast turned crazy. Go thou, daughter, quickly, and fetch a drink for thy father." His daughter went, and in the same way so it happened to her. She never thought till now that she was so lovable, and she took herself home. "Up with the drink," said her father. "Thou homespun shoe carle, dost thou think that I am fit to be thy thrall." The poor shoemaker thought that they had taken a turn in their understandings, and he went himself to the well. He saw the shadow of the maiden in the well, and he looked up to the tree, and he sees the finest woman he ever saw. "Thy seat is wavering, but thy face is fair," said the shoemaker. "Come down, for there is need of thee for a short while at my house." The shoemaker under-

24

stood that this was the shadow that had driven his people *Scotch*
mad.

The shoemaker took her to his house, and he said that
he had but a poor bothy, but that she should get a share
of all that was in it. At the end of a day or two came
a leash of gentlemen lads to the shoemaker's house for
shoes to be made for them, for the king's son had come
home, and he was going to marry. At a glance the
lads saw the giant's daughter, and they never saw one
so pretty as she. " 'Tis thou hast the pretty daughter
here," said the lads to the shoemaker. " She is pretty
indeed," says the shoemaker, " but she is no daughter
of mine." " St. Nail ! " said one of them, " I would give
a hundred pounds to marry her." The two others said the
very same. The poor shoemaker said that he had nothing
to do with her. " But," said they, " ask her to-night, and
send us word to-morrow." When the gentles went away,
she asked the shoemaker : " What's that they were saying
about me ? " The shoemaker told her. " Go thou after
them," said she ; " I will marry one of them, and let him
bring his purse with him." The youth returned and he
gave the shoemaker a hundred pounds for tocher. They
went to rest, and when she had laid down, she asked the
lad for a drink of water from a tumbler that was on the
board on the farther side of the chamber. He went ; but
out of that he could not come, as he held the vessel of water
the length of the night. " Thou lad," said she, " why wilt
thou not lie down ? " But out of that he could not drag till
the bright morrow's day was. The shoemaker came to
the door of the chamber, and she asked him to take away
that lubberly boy. This wooer went and betook himself
to his home, but he did not tell the other two how it happened
to him. Next came the second chap, and in the same way,
when she had gone to rest, " Look," she said, " if the latch
is on the door." The latch laid hold of his hands, and out

25

Scotch of that he could not come the length of the night, and out of that he did not come till the morrow's day was bright. He went, under shame and disgrace. No matter, he did not tell the other chap how it had happened, and on the third night he came. As it happened to the two others, so it happened to him. One foot stuck to the floor ; he could neither come nor go, but so he was the length of the night. On the morrow, he took his soles out of that, and he was not seen looking behind him. " Now," said the girl to the shoemaker, " thine is the sporran of gold ; I have no need of it. It will better thee, and I am no worse for thy kindness to me." The shoemaker had the shoes ready, and on that very day the king's son was to be married. The shoemaker was going to the castle with the shoes of the young people, and the girl said to the shoemaker : " I would like to get a sight of the king's son before he marries." " Come with me," says the shoemaker. " I am well acquainted with the servants of the castle, and thou shalt get a sight of the king's son and all the company." And when the gentles saw the pretty woman that was here they took her to the wedding-room, and they filled for her a glass of wine. When she was going to drink what was in it, a flame went up out of the glass, and a golden pigeon and a silver pigeon sprang out of it. They were flying about when three grains of barley fell on the floor. The silver pigeon sprang, and he eats that. Said the golden pigeon to him : " If thou hadst mind when I cleared the byre, thou wouldst not eat that without giving me a share." Again fell three other grains of barley, and the silver pigeon sprang, and he eats that, as before. " If thou hadst mind when I thatched the byre, thou wouldst not eat that without giving me my share," says the golden pigeon. Three other grains fell, and the silver pigeon sprang, and he eats that. " If thou hadst mind when I harried the magpie's nest, thou wouldst not eat that without giving me my share," says the golden pigeon ; " I lost my

26

" *If thou wilt give me this pretty little one,*"
says the king's son, " *I will take thee at*
thy word "

*And thereupon King Lludd went after
him and spoke unto him thus : " Stop,
stop," said he*

little finger bringing it down, and I want it still." The *Scotch* king's son minded, and he knew whom it was he had got. He sprang where she was, and kissed her from hand to mouth. And when the priest came they married a second time. And there I left them.

LLUDD AND LLEVELYS

BELI the Great, the son of Manogan, had three sons, Lludd, and Caswallawn, and Nynyaw ; and according to the story he had a fourth son called Llevelys. And after the death of Beli, the kingdom of the Island of Britain fell into the hands of Lludd his eldest son ; and Lludd ruled prosperously, and rebuilt the walls of London, and encompassed it about with numberless towers. And after that he bade the citizens build houses therein, such as no houses in the kingdoms could equal. And moreover he was a mighty warrior, and generous and liberal in giving meat and drink to all that sought them. And though he had many castles and cities this one loved he more than any. And he dwelt therein most part of the year, and therefore was it called Caer Lludd, and at last Caer London. And after the stranger-race came there, it was called London, or Lwndrys.

Lludd loved Llevelys best of all his brothers, because he was a wise and discreet man. Having heard that the King of France had died, leaving no heir except a daughter, and that he had left all his possessions in her hands, he came to Lludd his brother to beseech his counsel and aid. And that not so much for his own welfare as to seek to add to the glory and honour and dignity of his kindred, if he might go to France to woo the maiden for his wife. And forthwith his brother conferred with him, and this counsel was pleasing unto him.

28

So he prepared ships and filled them with armed knights, *Welsh* and set forth towards France. And as soon as they had landed they sent messengers to show the nobles of France the cause of the embassy. And by the joint counsel of the nobles of France and of the princes, the maiden was given to Llevelys, and the crown of the kingdom with her. And thenceforth he ruled the land discreetly, and wisely, and happily, as long as his life lasted.

After a space of time had passed, three plagues fell on the Island of Britain, such as none in the islands had ever seen the like of. The first was a certain race that came, and was called the Coranians ; and so great was their knowledge that there was no discourse upon the face of the island, however low it might be spoken, but what, if the wind met it, it was known to them. And through this they could not be injured. And their coin was fairy money—the money of the little people : that is money which, when received, appears to be good coin, but which, if kept, turns into pieces of fungus, or stones, or other rubbish.

The second plague was a shriek which came on every May-eve, over every hearth in the Island of Britain. And this went through people's hearts, and so scared them that the men lost their hue and their strength, and the women their children, and the young men and the maidens lost their senses, and all the animals and trees and the earth and the waters were left barren.

The third plague was that however much of provisions and food might be prepared in the king's courts, were there even so much as a year's provision of meat and drink, none of it could ever be found, except what was consumed in the first night. And two of these plagues, no one ever knew their cause, therefore was there better hope of being freed from the first than from the second and third.

And thereupon King Lludd felt great sorrow and care, because that he knew not how he might be freed from these

Welsh plagues. And he called to him all the nobles of his kingdom, and asked counsel of them what they should do against these afflictions. And by the common counsel of the nobles, Lludd the son of Beli went to Llevelys his brother, King of France, for he was a man great of counsel and wisdom, to seek his advice.

And they made ready a fleet, and that in secret and in silence, lest that race should know the cause of their errand, or any besides the king and his counsellors. And when they were made ready, they went into their ships, Lludd and those whom he chose with him. And they began to cleave the seas towards France.

And when these tidings came to Llevelys, seeing that he knew not the cause of his brother's ships, he came on the other side to meet him, and with him was a fleet vast of size. And when Lludd saw this, he left all the ships out upon the sea except one only ; and in that one he came to meet his brother, and he likewise with a single ship came to meet him. And when they were come together, each put his arms about the other's neck, and they welcomed each other with brotherly love.

After that Lludd had shown his brother the cause of his errand, Llevelys said that he himself knew the cause of the coming to those lands. And they took counsel together to discourse on the matter otherwise than thus, in order that the wind might not catch their words, nor the Coranians know what they might say. Then Llevelys caused a long horn to be made of brass, and through this horn they discoursed. But whatsoever words they spoke through this horn, one to the other, neither of them could hear any other but harsh and hostile words. And when Llevelys saw this, and that there was a demon thwarting them and disturbing through this horn, he caused wine to be put therein to wash it. And through the virtue of the wine the demon was driven out of the horn. And when their discourse was unobstructed

30

Llevelys told his brother that he would give him some *Welsh* insects whereof he should keep some to breed, lest by chance the like affliction might come a second time. And other of these insects he should take and bruise in water. And he assured him that it would have power to destroy the race of the Coranians. That is to say, that when he came home to his kingdom he should call together all the people both of his own race and of the race of the Coranians for a conference, as though with the intent of making peace between them ; and that when they were all together, he should take this charmed water, and cast it over all alike. And he assured him that the water would poison the race of the Coranians, but that it would not slay or harm those of his own race.

" And the second plague," said he, " that is in thy dominion, behold it is a dragon. And another dragon of a foreign race is fighting with it, and striving to overcome it. And therefore does your dragon make a fearful outcry. And on this wise mayest thou come to know this. After thou hast returned home, cause the island to be measured in its length and breadth, and in the place where thou dost find the exact central point, there cause a pit to be dug, and cause a cauldron full of the best mead that can be made to be put in the pit, with a covering of satin over the face of the cauldron. And then, in thine own person do thou remain there watching, and thou wilt see the dragon fighting in the form of terrific animals. And at length they will take the form of dragons in the air. And last of all, after wearying themselves with fierce and furious fighting, they will fall in the form of two pigs upon the covering, and they will sink in, and the covering with them, and they will draw it down to the very bottom of the cauldron. And they will drink up the whole of the mead ; and after that they will sleep. Thereupon do thou immediately fold the covering around them, and bury them in a kistvaen, in the strongest

31

Welsh place thou hast in thy dominions, and hide them in the earth. And as long as they shall bide in that strong place no plague shall come to the Island of Britain from elsewhere.

"The cause of the third plague," said he, "is a mighty man of magic, who takes thy meat and thy drink and thy store. And he through illusions and charms causes every one to sleep. Therefore it is needful for thee in thy own person to watch thy food and thy provisions. And lest he should overcome thee with sleep, be there a cauldron of cold water by thy side, and when thou art oppressed with sleep, plunge into the cauldron."

Then Lludd returned back unto his land. And immediately he summoned to him the whole of his own race and of the Coranians. And as Llevelys had taught him, he bruised the insects in water, the which he cast over them all together, and forthwith it destroyed the whole tribe of the Coranians, without hurt to any of the Britons.

And some time after this, Lludd caused the island to be measured in its length and in its breadth. And in Oxford he found the central point, and in that place he caused the earth to be dug, and in that pit a cauldron to be set, full of the best mead that could be made, and a covering of satin over the face of it. And he himself watched that night. And while he was there, he beheld the dragons fighting. And when they were weary they fell, and came down upon the top of the satin, and drew it with them to the bottom of the cauldron. And when they had drunk the mead they slept. And in their sleep, Lludd folded the covering around them, and in the securest place he had in Snowdon, he hid them in a kistvaen. Now after that this spot was called Dinas Emreis, but before that, Dinas Ffaraon. And thus the fierce outcry ceased in his dominions.

And when this was ended, King Lludd caused an exceeding great banquet to be prepared. And when it was ready, he placed a vessel of cold water by his side, and he in his

32

own proper person watched it. And as he abode thus clad *Welsh* with arms, about the third watch of the night, lo, he heard many surpassing fascinations and various songs. And drowsiness urged him to sleep. Upon this, lest he should be hindered from his purpose and be overcome by sleep, he went often into the water. And at last, behold, a man of vast size, clad in strong, heavy armour, came in, bearing a hamper. And, as he was wont, he put all the food and provisions of meat and drink into the hamper, and proceeded to go with it forth. And nothing was ever more wonderful to Lludd than that the hamper should hold so much.

And thereupon King Lludd went after him and spoke unto him thus : " Stop, stop," said he ; " though thou hast done many insults and much spoil erewhile, thou shalt not do so any more, unless thy skill in arms and thy prowess be greater than mine."

Then the giant instantly put down the hamper on the floor and awaited the king. And a fierce encounter was between them, so that the glittering fire flew out from their arms. And at the last Lludd grappled with him, and fate bestowed the victory on Lludd. And he threw the plague to the earth. And after he had overcome him by strength and might, he besought his mercy. " How can I grant thee mercy," said the king, " after all the many injuries and wrongs that thou hast done me ? " " All the losses that ever I have caused thee," said he, " I will make thee atonement for, equal to what I have taken. And I will never do the like from this time forth. But thy faithful vassal will I be." And the king accepted this from him.

And thus Lludd freed the Island of Britain from the three plagues. And from thenceforth until the end of his life, in prosperous peace did Lludd the son of Beli rule the Island of Britain. And this Tale is called the Story of Lludd and Llevelys. And thus it ends.

GULEESH

Irish

THERE was once a boy in the County Mayo, and Guleesh was his name, and there was the finest lis, or rath, in Ireland a little way off from the gable of the house where he lived, and he was often in the habit of seating himself on the fine grass bank that was running round it. One night he stood and half leaned against the gable of the house looking up into the sky, and watching the beautiful white moon over his head. After him to be standing that way for a couple of hours, he said to himself: "My bitter grief that I am not gone away out of this place altogether. I'd sooner be any place in the world than here. Och, it's well for you, white moon," says he, "that's turning round, turning round, as you please yourself, and no man can put you back. I wish I was the same as you."

Hardly was the word out of his mouth when he heard a great noise coming like the sound of many people running together, and talking and laughing and making sport, and the sound went by him like a whirl of wind, and he was listening to it going into the rath. "Musha, by my soul," says he, "but ye're merry enough, and I'll follow ye."

What was in the rath but the fairy host, though he did not know at first that it was they who were in it, but he

34

followed them into the rath. It's there he heard the *Irish*
fulparnee and the folpornee, the rap-lay-hoota and the
rollya-boolya that they had there, and every man of
them crying out as loud as he could : " My horse
and bridle and saddle ! My horse and bridle and
saddle ! "

" By my hand," said Guleesh, " my boy, that's not bad.
I'll imitate ye," and he cried out as well as they : " My
horse and bridle and saddle ! My horse and bridle and
saddle ! " And on the moment there was a fine horse,
with a bridle of gold and a saddle of silver, standing
before him. He leaped up on it, and the moment he
was on its back he saw clearly that the rath was full of
horses, and of little people going riding on them.

Said a man of them to him : " Are you coming with us
to-night, Guleesh ? "

" I am surely," said Guleesh.

" If you are, come along," said the little man, and
out with them altogether, riding like the wind, faster
than the fastest horse ever you saw a-hunting, and faster
than the fox and the hounds at his tail.

The cold winter's wind that was before them, they
overtook her, and the cold winter's wind that was behind
them, she did not overtake them. And stop nor stay of
that full race did they make none until they came to the
brink of the sea.

Then every one of them said : " Hie over cap ! Hie
over cap ! " and that moment they were up in the air,
and before Guleesh had time to remember where he was
they were down on dry land again, and were going like
the wind. At last they stood, and a man of them said
to Guleesh : " Guleesh, do you know where you are now ? "

" Now a know," said Guleesh.

" You're in Rome, Guleesh," said he ; " but we're
going farther than that. The daughter of the King of

35

Irish France is to be married to-night, the handsomest woman
that the sun ever saw, and we must do our best to bring
her with us, if we're only able to carry her off; and
you must come with us that we may be able to put the
young girl up behind you on the horse, when we'll be
bringing her away, for it's not lawful for us to put her
sitting behind ourselves. But you're flesh and blood, and
she can take a good grip of you, so that she won't fall off
the horse! Are you satisfied, Guleesh, and will you do
what we're telling you?"

"Why shouldn't I be satisfied?" said Guleesh. "I'm
satisfied, surely, and anything that ye will tell me to do I'll
do it without doubt; but tell me, where are we going?"

"We're to go to the palace of the King of France," said
they; "and if we can at all, we're to carry off his daughter
with us."

Every man of them then said, "Rise up, horse"; and the
horses began leaping and running and prancing.

The cold wind of winter that was before them they overtook her, and the cold wind of winter that was behind them,
she did not overtake them, and they never stopped of that
race till they came as far as the palace of the King of France.

They got off their horses there, and a man of them said a
word that Guleesh did not understand, and on the moment
they were lifted up, and Guleesh found himself and his
companions in the palace. There was a great feast going
on there, and there was not a nobleman or a gentleman in
the kingdom but was gathered there, dressed in silk and
satin and gold and silver, and the night was as bright as
the day with all the lamps and candles that were lit, and
Guleesh had to shut his two eyes at the brightness. When
he opened them again and looked from him, he thought he
never saw anything as fine as all he saw there. There were
a hundred tables spread out, and their full of meat and drink
on each table of them, flesh-meat and cakes and sweetmeats,
36

and wine and ale, and every drink that ever a man saw. *Irish*
The musicians were at the two ends of the hall, and they
playing the sweetest music that ever a man's ear heard,
and there were young women and fine youths in the middle
of the hall, dancing and turning, and going round so
quickly and lightly that it made Guleesh giddy to be
looking at them. There were more there playing tricks,
and more making fun and laughing, for such a feast as
there was that day had not been in France for twenty years,
because the old king had no children alive but only the
one daughter, and she was to be married to the son of another
king that night. Three days the feast was going on, and
the third night she was to be married, and that was
the night that Guleesh and the fairies came, hoping,
if they could, to carry off with them the king's young
daughter.

Guleesh and his companions were standing together at
the head of the hall, where there was a fine altar dressed up,
and two bishops behind it waiting to marry the girl as
soon as the right time should come. Nobody could see
the fairies, for they said a word as they came in that made
them all invisible, as if they had not been there at all.

"Tell me which of them is the king's daughter," said
Guleesh, when he was becoming a little used to the noise
and the light.

"Don't you see her there from you?" said the little man
that he was talking to.

Guleesh looked where the little man was pointing with
his finger, and there he saw the loveliest woman that was,
he thought, upon the ridge of the world. The rose and the
lily were fighting together in her face, and one could not
tell which of them got the victory. Her arms and hands
were like lime-blossom, her mouth as red as a strawberry
when it is ripe, her foot was as small and as light as another
one's hand, her form was smooth and slender, and her hair

37

Irish was falling down from her head in buckles of gold. Her garments and dress were woven with gold and silver, and the bright stone that was in the ring on her hand was as shining as the sun.

Guleesh was nearly blinded with all the loveliness and beauty that was in her; but when he looked again he saw that she was crying, and that there was the trace of tears in her eyes. " It can't be," said Guleesh, " that there's grief on her, when everybody round her is so full of sport and merriment."

" Musha, then, she is grieved," said the little man; " for it's against her own will she's marrying, and she has no love for the husband she is to marry. The king was going to give her to him three years ago, when she was only fifteen, but she said she was too young, and requested him to leave her as she was yet. The king gave her a year's grace, and when that year was up he gave her another year's grace, and then another; but a week or a day he would not give her longer, and she is eighteen years old to-night, and it's time for her to marry; but, indeed," says he, and he crooked his mouth in an ugly way, " indeed, it's no king's son she'll marry if I can help it."

Guleesh pitied the handsome young lady greatly when he heard that, and he was heart-broken to think that it would be necessary for her to marry a man she did not like, or, what was worse, to take a nasty fairy for a husband. However, he did not say a word, though he could not help giving many a curse to the ill-luck that was laid out for himself, and he helping the people that were to snatch her away from her home and from her father.

He began thinking, then, what it was he ought to do to save her, but he could think of nothing. " Oh, if I could only give her some help and relief," said he, " I wouldn't care whether I were alive or dead; but I see nothing that I can do for her."

38

GULEESH

He was looking on when the king's son came up to her *Irish* and asked her for a kiss, but she turned her head away from him. Guleesh had double pity for her then, when he saw the lad taking her by the soft white hand and drawing her out to dance. They went round in the dance near where Guleesh was, and he could plainly see that there were tears in her eyes.

When the dancing was over, the old king, her father, and her mother the queen, came up and said that this was the right time to marry her, that the bishop was ready and the couch prepared, and it was time to put the wedding-ring on her and give her to her husband.

The old king put a laugh out of him : " Upon my honour," he said, " the night is nearly spent, but my son will make a night for himself. I'll go bail he won't rise early to-morrow."

" Musha, and maybe he would," said the fairy in Guleesh's ear, " or not go to bed, perhaps, at all. Ha, ha, ha ! "

Guleesh gave him no answer, for his two eyes were starting out of his head watching to see what they would do then.

The king took the youth by the hand, and the queen took her daughter, and they went up together to the altar, with the lords and great people following them.

When they came near the altar, and were no more than about four yards from it, the little fairy stretched out his foot before the girl, and she fell. Before she was able to rise again he threw something that was in his hand upon her, said a couple of words, and upon the moment the maiden was gone from amongst them. Nobody could see her, for that word made her invisible. The little maneen seized her and raised her up behind Guleesh, and the king nor no one else saw them, but out with them through the hall till they came to the door.

Oro ! dead Mary ! it's there the pity was, and the trouble, and the crying, and the wonder, and the searching, and the rookaun, when that lady disappeared from their eyes, and

39

Irish without their seeing what did it. Out on the door of the palace with them without being stopped or hindered, for nobody saw them, and " My horse and bridle and saddle ! " says every man of them.

" My horse and bridle and saddle ! " says Guleesh ; and on the moment the horse was standing ready caparisoned before him. " Now, jump up, Guleesh," said the little man, " and put the lady behind you, and we will be going ; the morning is not far off from us now."

Guleesh raised her up on the horse's back, and leaped up himself before her, and " Rise horse," said he ; and his horse, and the other horses with him, went in a full race until they came to the sea.

" Hie over cap ! " said every man of them.

" Hie over cap ! " said Guleesh ; and on the moment the horse rose under him and cut a leap in the clouds, and came down in Erin.

They did not stop, but went of a race to the place where was Guleesh's house and the rath. And when they came as far as that, Guleesh turned and caught the young girl in his two arms, and leaped off the horse.

" I call and cross you to myself, in the name of God ! " said he ; and on the spot, before the word was out of his mouth, the horse fell down, and what was in it but the beam of a plough, of which they had made a horse ; and every other horse they had, it was that way they made it. Some of them were riding on an old besom, and some on a broken stick, and more on a ragweed or a hemlock-stalk.

The good people called out together when they heard what Guleesh said :

" Oh, Guleesh, you clown, you thief, that no good may happen you. Why did you play that trick on us ? "

But they had no power at all to carry off the girl after Guleesh had consecrated her to himself.

" Oh, Guleesh, isn't that a nice turn you did us, and we

40

so kind to you ?   What good have we now out of our journey *Irish*
to Rome and to France ?   Never mind yet, you clown, but
you'll pay us another time for this.   Believe us, you'll
repent it."

"He'll have no good to get out of the young girl," said
the little man that was talking to him in the palace before
that, and as he said the word he moved over to her and
struck her a slap on the side of the head.   " Now," says he,
" she'll be without talk any more ; now, Guleesh, what
good will she be to you when she'll be dumb ?   It's time for
us to go—but you'll remember us, Guleesh ! "

When he said that he stretched out his two hands, and
before Guleesh was able to give an answer he and the rest
of them were gone into the rath out of his sight, and he saw
them no more.

He turned to the young woman and said to her : "Thanks
be to God, they're gone.   Would you not sooner stay with
me than with them ? "   She gave him no answer.   " There's
trouble and grief on her yet," said Guleesh in his own mind,
and he spoke to her again : " I am afraid that you must
spend this night in my father's house, lady, and if there is
anything that I can do for you, tell me, and I'll be your
servant."

The beautiful girl remained silent, but there were tears
in her eyes, and her face was white and red after each other.

"Lady," said Guleesh, " tell me what you would like me
to do now.   I never belonged at all to that lot of fairies
who carried you away with them.   I am the son of an honest
farmer, and I went with them without knowing it.   If I'll
be able to send you back to your father I'll do it, and I pray
you make any use of me now that you may wish."

He looked into her face, and he saw the mouth moving
as if she were going to speak, but there came no word
from it.

"It cannot be," said Guleesh, " that you are dumb.   Did

Irish I not hear you speaking to the king's son in the palace to-night? Or has that devil really made you dumb, when he struck his nasty hand on your jaw?"

The girl raised her white, smooth hand, and laid her finger on her tongue, to show him that she had lost her voice and power of speech, and the tears ran out of her two eyes like streams, and Guleesh's own eyes were not dry, for, as rough as he was on the outside, he had a soft heart, and could not stand the sight of the young girl, and she in that unhappy plight.

He began thinking with himself what he ought to do, and he did not like to bring her home with himself to his father's house, for he knew well that they would not believe him, that he had been in France and brought back with him the King of France's daughter, and he was afraid they might make a mock of the young lady or insult her.

At last he thought : " I know now what I'll do ; I'll bring her to the priest's house, and he won't refuse me to keep the lady and care for her." He turned to the lady again and told her that he was loath to take her to his father's house, but that there was an excellent priest, very friendly to himself, who would take good care of her if she wished to remain in his house ; but that if there was any other place to which she would rather go, he said he would bring her to it.

She bent her head, to show him she was obliged, and gave him to understand that she was ready to follow him anywhere. "We will go to the priest's house then," said he ; " he is under an obligation to me, and will do anything I ask him."

They went together accordingly to the priest's house, and the sun was just rising when they came to the door. Guleesh beat it hard, and as early as it was the priest was up, and opened the door himself. He wondered when he saw Guleesh

42

*The dragon flew out and caught the queen
on the road and carried her away*

"Now, Guleesh, what good will she be to
you when she'll be dumb? It's time for
us to go—but you'll remember us, Guleesh!"

and the girl, for he was certain that it was coming wanting *Irish*
to be married they were.

"Guleesh, isn't it the nice boy you are that you can't
wait until ten o'clock or till twelve, but that you must be
coming to me at this hour looking for marriage, you and
your bride. But ubbubboo!" said he suddenly, as he
looked again at the young girl; "in the name of God,
who have you here? Who is she, or how did you get
her?"

Then Guleesh told him that she was the daughter of the
King of France.

The priest looked at him as though he had ten heads on
him; but, without putting any other question to him, he
desired him to come in, himself and the maiden, and when
they came in he shut the door, brought them into the parlour,
and put them sitting.

"Now, Guleesh," said he, "tell me truly who is this
young lady, and whether you're out of your senses really
or are only making a joke of me?"

"I'm not telling a word of a lie, nor making a joke of
you," said Guleesh; "but it was from the palace of the
King of France I carried off this lady, and she is the
daughter of the King of France."

He began his story then, and told the whole to the priest,
and the priest was so much surprised that he could not help
calling out at times or clapping his hands together.

When Guleesh said from what he saw he thought the
girl was not satisfied with the marriage that was going to
take place in the palace before he and the fairies broke
it up, there came a red blush into the girl's cheek, and he
was more certain than ever that she had sooner be as she
was—badly as she was—than be the married wife of the
man she hated. When Guleesh said that he would be very
thankful to the priest if he would keep her in his own house,
the kind man said he would do that as long as Guleesh

Irish pleased, but that he did not know what they ought to do with her, because they had no means of sending her back to her father again.

Guleesh answered that he was uneasy about the same thing, and that he saw nothing to do but to keep quiet until they should find some opportunity of doing something better. They made it up then between themselves that the priest should let on that it was his brother's daughter he had, who was come on a visit to him from another country, and that he should tell everybody that she was dumb, and do his best to keep every one away from her. They told the young girl what it was they intended to do, and she showed by her eyes that she was obliged to them.

Guleesh went home then, and when his people asked him where he had been he said that he fell asleep at the foot of the ditch and passed the night there.

There was great wonderment on the neighbours at the girl who came so suddenly to the priest's house without any one knowing where she was from, or what business she had there. And there were some of them who said that Guleesh was not like the same man he had been before, and that it was a thing to wonder at how he was drawing every day to the priest's house.

That was true for them, indeed, for it was seldom the day went by but Guleesh would go to the priest's house and have a talk with him, and as often as he would come he used to hope to find the young lady well again, and with leave to speak ; but, alas, she remained dumb and silent, without relief or cure. Since she had no other means of talking, she carried on a sort of conversation between herself and Guleesh by moving her hand and fingers, winking her eyes, opening and shutting her mouth, laughing or smiling, and a thousand other signs, so that it was not long until they understood each other very well. Guleesh was always thinking how he should send her back to her father ; but

44

there was no one to go with her, and he himself did not *Irish*
know what road to go, for he had never been out of his own
country before the night he brought her away with him.
Nor had the priest any better knowledge than he ; but when
Guleesh asked him, he wrote three or four letters to the
King of France, and gave them to buyers and sellers of
wares, who used to be going from place to place across the
sea ; but they all went astray, and never one came to the
king's hand.

This was the way they were for many months, and Guleesh
was falling deeper and deeper in love with her every day,
and it was plain to himself and the priest that she liked him.
The boy feared greatly at last lest the king should really
hear where his daughter was and take her back from himself,
and he besought the priest to write no more, but to leave
the matter to God.

So they passed the time for a year, until there came
a day when Guleesh was lying by himself on the grass,
on the last day of the last full month of autumn, and he
thinking over again in his own mind of everything that
happened to him from the day that he went with the fairies
across the sea. He remembered then, suddenly, that it
was one November night that he was standing at the gable
of the house, when the whirlwind came, and the fairies
in it, and he said to himself : " We have a November night
again to-day, and I'll stand in the same place I was in last
year, until I see if the good people come again. Perhaps
I might see or hear something that would be useful to me,
and might bring back her talk again to Mary "—that was
the name himself and the priest called the king's daughter,
for neither of them knew her right name. He told his
intention to the priest, and the priest gave him his
blessing.

Guleesh accordingly went to the old rath when the night
was darkening, and he stood with his elbow leaning on

Irish a grey old flag, waiting till the middle of the night should come. The moon rose slowly, and it was like a knob of fire behind him ; and there was a white fog which was raised up over the fields of grass and all damp places, through the coolness of the night after a great heat in the day. The night was calm as is a lake when there is not a breath of wind to move a wave on it, and there was no sound to be heard but the hum of the insects that would go by from time to time, or the hoarse, sudden scream of the wild geese as they passed from lake to lake, half a mile up in the air over his head ; or the sharp whistle of the golden and green plovers, rising and lying, lying and rising, as they do on a calm night. There were a thousand thousand bright stars shining over his head, and there was a little frost out, which left the grass under his foot white and crisp.

He stood there for an hour, for two hours, for three hours, and the frost increased greatly, so that he heard the breaking of the traneens under his foot as often as he moved. He was thinking, in his own mind, at last that the fairies would not come that night, and that it was as good for him to return again, when he heard a sound far away from him, coming towards him, and he recognized what it was at the first moment. The sound increased, and at first it was like the beating of waves on a stony shore, and then it was like the falling of a great waterfall, and at last it was like a loud storm in the tops of the trees, and then the whirlwind burst into the rath at one rout, and the fairies were in it.

It all went by him so suddenly that he lost his breath with it, but he came to himself on the spot, and put an ear on himself, listening to what they would say. Scarcely had they gathered into the rath till they all began shouting and screaming and talking amongst themselves ; and then each one of them cried out : " My horse and bridle and saddle !

46

My horse and bridle and saddle!" and Guleesh took courage *Irish*
and called out as loudly as any of them : " My horse and
bridle and saddle ! My horse and bridle and saddle !" But
before the word was well out of his mouth another man
cried out : " Oro ! Guleesh, my boy, are you here with us
again ? How are you coming on with your woman ?
There's no use in your calling for your horse to-night. I'll
go bail you won't play on us again. It was a good trick you
played on us last year !"

" It was," said another man ; " he won't do it again."

" Isn't he a prime lad, the same lad, to take a woman with
him that never said as much to him as ' How do you do ? '
since this time last year !" says the third man.

" Perhaps he likes to be looking at her," said another
voice.

" And if the omadawn only knew that there's a herb
growing up by his own door, and to boil it and give it to
her, and she'd be well !" said another voice.

" That's true for you."

" He is an omadawn."

" Don't bother your head with him, we'll be going."

" We'll leave the bodach as he is."

And with that they rose up into the air, and out with
them at one roolya-boolya the way they came ; and they
left poor Guleesh standing where they found him, and the
two eyes going out of his head, looking after them and
wondering.

He did not stand long till he turned back, and he thinking
in his own mind on all he saw and heard, and wondering
whether there was really a herb at his own door that
would bring back the talk to the king's daughter. " It
can't be," says he to himself, " that they would tell it to me
if there was any virtue in it ; but perhaps the fairy didn't
observe himself when he let the word slip out of his mouth.
I'll search well as soon as the sun rises, whether there's

Irish any plant growing beside the house except thistles and dockings."

He went home, and as tired as he was he did not sleep a wink until the sun rose on the morrow. He got up then, and it was the first thing he did to go out and search well through the grass round about the house, trying could he get any herb that he did not recognize. And, indeed, he was not long searching till he observed a large strange herb that was growing up just by the gable of the house.

He went over to it and observed it closely, and saw that there were seven little branches coming out of the stalk and seven leaves growing on every brancheen of them, and that there was a white sap in the leaves. " It's very wonderful," said he to himself, " that I never noticed this herb before. If there's any virtue in a herb at all, it ought to be in such a strange one as this."

He drew out his knife, cut the plant, and carried it into his own house ; stripped the leaves off it and cut up the stalk ; and there came a thick, white juice out of it, as there comes out of the sow-thistle when it is bruised, except that the juice was more like oil.

He put it in a little pot and a little water in it, and laid it on the fire until the water was boiling, and then he took a cup, filled it half up with the juice, and put it to his own mouth. It came into his head then that perhaps it was poison that was in it, and that the good people were only tempting him that he might kill himself with that trick, or put the girl to death without meaning it. He put down the cup again, raised a couple of drops on the top of his finger, and put it to his mouth. It was not bitter, and, indeed, had a sweet, agreeable taste. He grew bolder then, and drank the full of a thimble of it, and then as much again, and he never stopped till he had half the cup drunk. He fell asleep after that and did not wake

48

till it was night, and there was great hunger and great *Irish* thirst on him.

He had to wait, then, till the day rose ; but he determined, as soon as he should wake in the morning, that he would go to the king's daughter and give her a drink of the juice of the herb.

As soon as he got up in the morning he went over to the priest's house with the drink in his hand, and he never felt himself so bold and valiant, and spirited and light, as he was that day, and he was quite certain that it was the drink he drank which made him so hearty.

When he came to the house he found the priest and the young lady within, and they were wondering greatly why he had not visited them for two days.

He told them all his news, and said that he was certain that there was great power in that herb, and that it would do the lady no hurt, for he tried it himself and got good from it, and then he made her taste it, for he vowed and swore that there was no harm in it.

Guleesh handed her the cup, and she drank half of it, and then fell back on her bed and a heavy sleep came on her, and she never woke out of that sleep till the day on the morrow.

Guleesh and the priest sat up the entire night with her, waiting till she should awake, and they between hope and unhope, between expectation of saving her and fear of hurting her.

She awoke at last when the sun had gone half its way through the heavens. She rubbed her eyes and looked like a person who did not know where she was. She was like one astonished when she saw Guleesh and the priest in the same room with her, and she sat up doing her best to collect her thoughts.

The two men were in great anxiety waiting to see would she speak or would she not speak, and when they remained

49

Irish silent for a couple of minutes the priest said to her : " Did you sleep well, Mary ? "

And she answered him : " I slept, thank you."

No sooner did Guleesh hear her talking than he put a shout of joy out of him, and ran over to her, and fell on his two knees and said : " A thousand thanks to God, who has given you back the talk ; lady of my heart, speak again to me."

The lady answered him that she understood it was he who boiled that drink for her and gave it to her ; that she was obliged to him from her heart for all the kindness he showed her since the day she first came to Ireland, and that he might be certain that she never would forget it.

Guleesh was ready to die with satisfaction and delight. Then they brought her food, and she ate with a good appetite, and was merry and joyous, and never left off talking with the priest while she was eating.

After that Guleesh went home to his house, and stretched himself on the bed and fell asleep again, for the force of the herb was not all spent, and he passed another day and a night sleeping. When he woke up he went back to the priest's house, and found that the young lady was in the same state, and that she had been asleep almost from the time that he left the house.

He went into her chamber with the priest, and they remained watching beside her till she awoke the second time, and she had her talk as well as ever, and Guleesh was greatly rejoiced. The priest put food on the table again, and they ate together, and Guleesh used after that to come to the house from day to day, and the friendship that was between him and the king's daughter increased, because she had no one to speak to except Guleesh and the priest, and she liked Guleesh best, and was never tired of listening to him.

When they had been that way for another half-year she

said that she could stay no longer, but must go back to *Irish* her father and mother ; that she was certain that they were greatly grieved for her ; and that it was a shame for her to leave them in grief when it was in her power to go as far as them. The priest did all he could to keep her with them for another while, but without effect, and Guleesh spoke every sweet word that came into his head, trying to get the victory over her, and to coax her and make her stay as she was, but it was no good for him. She determined that she would go, and no man alive would make her change her intention.

She had not much money, but only two rings that were on her hand, when the fairy carried her away, and a gold pin that was in her hair, and golden buckles that were on her little shoes.

The priest took and sold them and gave her the money, and she said that she was ready to go.

She left her blessing and farewell with the priest and Guleesh, and departed. She was not long gone before there came such grief and melancholy over Guleesh that he knew he would not be long alive unless he were near her, and he followed her.

It was well, and it was not ill. They married one another, and that was the fine wedding they had, and had I been there then, I would not be here now ; but I heard it from a birdeen that there was neither cark nor care, sickness nor sorrow, mishap nor misfortune on them till the hour of their death, and that it may be the same with me, and with us all !

THE SLEEPING BEAUTY

French　ONCE upon a time there lived a king and queen who were in great trouble because they had no children. They were sorrier about it than words can tell. They offered up prayers, made vows and pilgrimages, moved heaven and earth—and for a long time it all seemed to be of no use. At last, however, their wish was granted, and the queen became the mother of a baby-girl. Such a fine christening was never seen before. All the fairies who could be found in the country —there were seven of them—were invited as godmothers of the little princess. As each one was bound to bring a fairy-gift—this being the custom with the fairies of those times—it stood to reason that the princess would have everything you could think of to make her perfectly good and beautiful and happy.

After the christening was over, the whole company went back to the king's palace, where there was a great festival in honour of the fairies. A magnificent banquet was spread for them, and in front of each fairy was set a solid gold casket, holding a knife and fork and spoon of beaten gold, studded with diamonds and rubies. But, as they all took their places at the table, along came an old fairy who had not been asked to the feast, because for the last fifty years she had never come out of the tower in which she lived, and everybody believed her either dead or under some spell.

THE SLEEPING BEAUTY

The king ordered that a place should be laid for her ; *French* but there was no means of giving her a solid gold casket like those that had been put before the others, because only seven had been made for the seven fairies who were expected. The old crone fancied herself slighted, and muttered some threat or other between her teeth. Now, one of the young fairies, who happened to be near, heard this, and guessing that the old fairy might revenge herself by dowering the little princess with some piece of ill-luck, she hid herself behind the tapestries as soon as the company had risen from the table. She did this so that she might be the last to speak, and could repair as far as possible any evil that the old fairy might be intending.

Meanwhile the fairies began to bestow their gifts upon the princess. The youngest promised, as her gift, that the princess should be the most beautiful woman in the world ; the next, that she should be cleverer than any mere mortal could hope to be ; the third, that whatever she should set her hand to she should do it with the most exquisite grace ; the fourth, that she should dance divinely ; the fifth, that she should sing like a nightingale ; and the sixth, that she should be complete mistress of every sort of musical instrument. Then came the old fairy's turn. Shaking her head—more through spite than through age—she said that the princess would one day prick her hand with a spindle, and die forthwith.

This terrible prophecy made the whole company shudder, and there was no one there who did not feel ready to cry. Just in the nick of time, the young fairy came out from behind the tapestry. "Reassure yourselves, king and queen!" said she, speaking at the top of her voice ; "your daughter shall not die. It is true that I have not the power to prevent altogether what my old friend has decreed. The princess will, indeed, prick her hand with a spindle ; but, instead of dying, she will only fall into a deep sleep which will last

French a hundred years, at the end of which time a king's son will come to wake her."

The king, who did all he could to ward off the doom pronounced by the old fairy, issued an edict forbidding any one to use a spindle, or even to have one in the house, on pain of death.

After fifteen or sixteen years, while the king and queen had gone to one of their pleasure-houses, it so fell out that the princess was playing in the castle, running through the rooms and climbing up stairway after stairway. At last she came to the very top of a turret, and found herself in a little garret, where an old woman sat all alone working with her spindle.

" What are you doing there, my good woman ? " said the princess. " I am spinning, my pretty child," answered the old lady, who did not appear to recognize her. " Oh ! how nice it looks," exclaimed the princess ; " how do you manage it ? Do give it me, and let me see if I can do it as well as you." No sooner had she taken the spindle, catching hold of it a little roughly in her eagerness—or perhaps it was only the decree of the fairies that ordained it so—than it pricked her hand, and she fell in a swoon to the ground.

The good old lady, who seemed in a great state of alarm, cried for help. From every side the servants came running. One of them threw water in the princess's face. Another loosened her collar. Another slapped her hands. Another bathed her forehead with Queen-of-Hungary water. But nothing would restore her.

Then the king, who had come back to the palace, and rushed upstairs as soon as he heard the noise, remembered the prophecy of the fairies. Judging shrewdly enough that this was bound to happen, since the fairies had said so, he had the princess put in the most beautiful room in the palace, upon a bed embroidered with gold and silver. You

would have said it was an angel lying there, so lovely was *French*
she, for her swoon had not robbed her complexion of its
glowing tints. Her cheeks were still rosy, and her lips like

"WHAT ARE YOU DOING THERE, MY
GOOD WOMAN?" SAID THE PRINCESS

coral. Her eyes were shut, but you could hear her soft
breathing, and see clearly enough that she was not dead.

He gave orders that the princess should be left to sleep
undisturbed until the time for her awakening should come.
The good fairy who had saved her life by dooming her to
sleep for a hundred years was in the kingdom of Mataquin,
twelve thousand leagues away, when the accident happened
to the princess ; but the news was soon brought to her
by a little dwarf, who had seven-league boots, so that he
could go seven leagues at each step. The fairy started off

French directly, and before an hour was over she had arrived, in her chariot of fire drawn by dragons, and had come down in the courtyard of the castle. The king went to her, and gave her his hand to help her out of the chariot. She approved of everything that he had done, but as she was very far-seeing, she thought that when the princess should come to wake she would be frightened at finding herself all alone in the old castle. What was to be done? How could this be avoided? The fairy soon found a way out of the difficulty.

She touched with her wand every one who was in the castle except the king and queen—governesses, ladies-in-waiting, chambermaids, courtiers, officers, stewards, cooks, scullions, errand-boys, guards, beadles, pages, footmen. She touched also all the horses that were in the stables—with the grooms—the big mastiffs in the stable-yard, and little "Puff," the princess's tiny lap-dog, who lay close to her on the bed. The very moment that she touched them they all went off to sleep also, not to wake until such time as their mistress should wake too, so that they could attend upon her when necessary. Even the spits which were turning at the fire, laden with partridges and pheasants—they went to sleep as well, and the very fire itself. The fairies did not take long over their work.

Then the king and queen, having kissed their much-loved daughter without waking her, left the castle, and published a proclamation that no one was to approach it, whoever they might be. The proclamation proved quite needless, for in a quarter of an hour there had grown all round the park such a vast number of trees, large and small, of brambles and of briars all intertwined one with the other, that neither man nor beast could have made a way through them. So thick and high was the growth that you could see nothing more than just the tips of the castle towers, and that only from a long way off. You may take it for granted

56

that this was another piece of the fairy's handiwork, and *French*
all arranged so that the princess, while she slept, should
have nothing to fear from inquisitive strangers.

At the end of a hundred years, the son of a king who was
reigning at that time, and who did not belong to the same
family as the sleeping princess, was hunting in the neigh-
bourhood, and asked what were those towers that he saw

peeping up above a dense forest. Every one told him just
what each had heard. Some said it was an old castle
haunted by spirits ; others that all the sorcerers in the
country gathered there to celebrate their rites. The most
common belief was that an ogre lived there, who carried
thither all the children he could lay hands on, and ate them
at his leisure, without any one being able to follow him,
because he alone was able to force his way through the
wood.

The prince was wondering what to think when a peasant
came forward. " Fifty years ago, my prince," said the
peasant, " my father told me that there was a princess in
the castle—the most beautiful princess ever seen—who was

57

French to sleep there for a hundred years. He told me, too, that she would be wakened by a king's son, whose bride she was destined to be."

When he heard this, the young prince was on fire with eagerness. Without worrying about any difficulties, he believed the adventure as good as accomplished, and, urged forward by thoughts of love and of glory, resolved to see straight away what was to be found there. Hardly had he reached the outskirts of the wood, when all the great trees, the brambles and the briars, parted of their own accord to let him pass through. He marched onwards to the castle, which he saw at the end of a great avenue, down which he duly made his way. It surprised him a little, however, to notice that none of his companions had been able to follow him, because the trees closed together again as soon as he had gone past. But a young man—and a prince and lover to boot—is ever valiant ! He did not allow himself to pause in his path, and soon came to a large outer court. Here everything that he cast his eye upon was of a sort to make his blood run cold. Over all was a fearful silence. The semblance of death met his gaze on every side—nothing but the stretched-out bodies of men and animals, all of them to every appearance dead. It was not long, however, before he recognized by the bulbous noses and still red faces of the porters that they were only asleep. Their glasses, where some drops of wine still lingered, served to show that they must have gone to sleep in the very act of drinking.

He passes a large court paved with marble. He mounts the staircase ; he enters the hall of the guards, who were drawn up in a row, their carbines on their shoulders, snoring for all they were worth. He goes through several rooms full of lords and ladies, all asleep, some upright, others sitting down. At last he enters a gilded room, where he saw upon a bed—the curtains of which were open at each side—the most beautiful sight that he had ever known, the

58

" *Art thou warm, maiden? Art thou warm, pretty one? Art thou warm, my darling?* "

*Nine peahens flew towards the tree. and
eight of them settled on its branches, but
the ninth alighted near him and turned
instantly into a beautiful girl*

figure of a young girl, who seemed to be about fifteen or *French*
sixteen years old. Her beauty seemed to shine with an
almost unearthly radiance. He drew near in trembling
wonder, and knelt down by her side.

Just then, as the end of her enchantment was come, the
princess woke, and looking at him with a glance more tender
than a moment's acquaintance would seem to warrant, " Is
it you, my prince? " said she. " How long you have kept
me waiting ! " The prince, charmed with these words, and
still more with the manner in which they were spoken, did
not know how to express his joy. He assured her that
he loved her more than himself. They did not use any fine
phrases, these two, but they were none the less happy on
that account. Where love is, what need of eloquence ? He
was more at a loss than she, and small wonder ! She had
had plenty of time to think over what she was going to say !
Anyhow, they talked together for four hours, and they had
not even then said half of what was in their hearts. " Can
it be, beautiful princess," said the prince, looking at her
with eyes that told a thousand things more than tongue
could utter, " can it be that some kindly fate ordained that
I should be born expressly for you ? Can it be that these
beautiful eyes only open for me—that all the kings of the
earth, with all their power, could not do what my love
has done ? " " Yes, my dear prince," replied the princess ;
" I knew at first sight that we were born for each other.
It is you that I saw, that I talked with, that I loved, all
through my long sleep. It was with your image that the
fairy filled my dreams. I knew that he who would come to
free me from my spell would be lovelier than love itself ;
that he would love me more than his own life ; and directly
you came to me, I recognized him in you."

In the meantime, everybody in the palace had woken up
at the same moment as the princess. Each began worrying
about his or her duties, and as they were not all lovers, they

French began to remember that it was a long time since they had had anything to eat, and that they were ready to die with hunger. The lady-in-waiting, as famished as the rest, grew impatient, and called to the princess that supper was ready. The prince helped the princess to get up. She was fully and very magnificently dressed; but he was careful not to remind her that her ruff and farthingale were after the fashion of his grandmother's time. She was none the less beautiful for that.

They passed into a saloon with mirrors all round the walls, and there they had supper. The musicians, with fiddles and hautboys, played some old pieces of music, excellent in their way, though a hundred years had gone by since they were heard last. After supper, without losing any time, the chief chaplain married the prince and princess in the chapel, and they retired to rest. They slept little. The princess, to be sure, after her hundred years, had no great need of sleep, and as soon as morning broke the prince left her, and returned to the town, for he knew the king his father would be growing anxious about him.

The prince told him that, when hunting, he had been lost in the forest, had spent the night in a charcoal-burners' hut, and had made his supper of black bread and cheese. The king his father, who was an easy-going fellow, believed him; but the queen his mother would not be so easily persuaded. She noticed that the prince was always going hunting, and seemed always to have some excuse or other for staying away several days; and she had a shrewd suspicion that he had a sweetheart somewhere or other. She often tried to get him to tell her all about it by hinting that he should be contented with life at the palace; but he never dared trust her with his secret. He feared her, although he loved her. For she came of a family of ogresses, and the king had only married her for her wealth. It used even to

60

be whispered at the court that she herself had all the instincts *French*
of an ogress, and that when she saw any little children
passing by she had to hold herself back to keep from rushing
at them. So the prince thought it best not to tell her anything at all. For two years he continued seeing his beloved
princess in secret, and he loved her always more and more.
The air of mystery about it all made him fall in love with her
afresh each time he saw her, and homely joys did not lessen
the warmth of his passion.

So when the king his father was dead, and he saw himself master, he declared his marriage publicly, and went
in full state to visit the queen his wife in her castle. It
was with all possible pomp and ceremony that he now
made his entry into what was, after all, the old capital of
the country.

Some time after he had become king, the prince went to
make war upon his neighbour, the Emperor Cantalabutte.
He left the management of the kingdom in the hands of the
queen his mother, and told her to be kind to the young
queen, whom he loved all the more since she had brought
him two pretty children—a girl and a boy—whom he called
Dawn and Day, because they were so beautiful. The king
was to be away at the war all the summer, and no sooner
had he gone than the queen-mother sent her daughter-
in-law and the children to a country house in the woods,
where she could more easily satisfy her horrible craving.
She went there herself some days afterwards, and said
one evening to her steward : " Master Simon, to-morrow I
mean to eat little Dawn for my dinner." " Oh, madam ! "
says the steward. " I wish it," replies the queen-mother,
in the tones of an ogress, hungry for fresh young victims.

The poor man, seeing that it would be no use trying to
thwart an ogress, took his big knife and went up to little
Dawn's room. She was just four years old, and she ran to
him, laughing and skipping, and threw her arms round his

French neck, and asked him if he had brought her some sweetstuff. The knife fell from his hands, and he went to the yard, and cut the throat of a little lamb instead. This he served up with some sauce, which was so delightful that the queen-mother vowed she had never tasted anything better in her life. In the meantime he carried off little Dawn, and gave her to his wife, who hid her in their own quarters at the bottom of the yard.

About a week afterwards, the wicked queen-mother said to her steward : " Master Simon, I want to eat little Day for my supper." He did not reply at all, but, resolving to deceive her again, went to look for little Day, and found him with a tiny foil in his hand, with which he was pretending to fence a huge ape. He was only three years old. The steward carried the boy to his wife, who hid him with little Dawn ; and he served up instead to the wicked queen-mother a tender little kid, which she found admirable fare. So all was well, so far as that was concerned ; but one evening the wicked old queen called out in a terrible voice : " Master Simon ! Master Simon ! " He went to her immediately. " To-morrow," said she, " I want to eat my daughter-in-law." Then at last Master Simon despaired of being still able to hoodwink the old ogress. The young queen was now some twenty years old, without counting the hundred years that she had slept. How should he get an animal to replace her ? He decided that there was nothing for it. To save his own life, he must cut the young queen's throat, and he went up to her room determined to finish the business there and then. Working himself up into a suitable frenzy, he entered the young queen's room. He did not wish, however, to take her altogether by surprise ; so with great respect he told her of the orders he had received from the queen-mother. " Kill me ! kill me ! " said she, offering him her neck ; " fulfil the command that has been given you. I shall only be going to see my children again—

my poor children, whom I loved so well!" She believed *French* them dead, as they had been taken away without anything having been said to her.

"No, no, madam!" replied poor Master Simon, his heart softening, "you shall not die. You shall go to see your dear children again ; but it shall be in my house, where I am keeping them in hiding. I will trick the old queen once more. I will make her eat a young hind in your place." He took her without more ado to his wife's room, where he left her clasping her children in her arms and crying with them, and went to prepare the hind, which the ogress ate for her supper with just as much gusto as if it had indeed been the young queen. She was, in fact, quite delighted over her own cruelty, and had made up her mind to tell the king when he came back that some ravenous wolves had eaten his wife and his two children.

One evening, while the old queen was roaming about the courts and yards of the castle to see if she could sniff out some fresh dainty, she heard in one of the back rooms little Day, who was crying because his mother was going to whip him for being naughty. She also heard little Dawn asking forgiveness for her brother. The ogress recognized the voices of the young queen and her children. Furious at having been duped, she commanded—in that terrible voice of hers that frightened everybody—that on the very next morning a huge tub should be brought into the middle of the court. It should be filled with toads, vipers, adders, and all sorts of reptiles, and the young queen and her children, Master Simon, his wife, and servant were all to be thrown in together. They were to be brought thither—so the old queen commanded—with their hands tied behind their backs.

They were already there—the executioners stood in readiness to throw them into the tub—when the young queen asked that at least she should be allowed to bid her children

French farewell, and the ogress, wicked as she was, consented. " Alas, alas ! " cried the poor princess, "must I die so young. It is true that I have been a good while in the world, but I have slept a hundred years, and surely that ought not to count ! What will you say, what will you do, my poor prince, when you come back, and find that your little Day, who is so sweet, and your little Dawn, who is so pretty, are there no longer to throw their little arms round your neck, and that even I myself am no longer there to greet you ? If I weep, it is your tears that I shed. Perhaps—I dread to think it—you will take vengeance for our fate upon yourself ! As for you, miserable wretches, who do an ogress's bidding, the king will have you put to death—burnt to death on a slow fire." The ogress, when she heard these words— which went so far beyond a mere farewell—was transported with rage, and cried : " Executioners, do your duty, and throw this babbler into the tub ! " They there and then approached the queen, and took hold of her by her dress ; but, just at that moment, the king, whom no one expected to arrive so early, came riding into the court. He had come post-haste ; and he asked, in his astonishment, what was the meaning of this horrible sight. No one dared to tell him ; when the ogress, maddened at seeing the course events had taken, threw herself head foremost into the tub, and was gobbled up in an instant by the dreadful creatures she had ordered to be put there. The king did not allow himself to be grieved over-much, although she was his mother. He soon found consolation in his beautiful wife and his children.

MORAL

Many a girl has waited long
For a husband brave or strong ;
But I'm sure I never met
Any sort of woman yet
Who could wait a hundred years,
Free from fretting, free from fears.

THE SLEEPING BEAUTY

Now, our story seems to show   *French*
That a century or so,
Late or early, matters not;
True love comes by fairy-lot.
Some old folk will even say
It grows better by delay.

Yet this good advice, I fear,
Helps us neither there nor here.
Though philosophers may prate
How much wiser 'tis to wait,
Maids will be a-sighing still—
Young blood must when young blood will.

CESARINO AND THE DRAGON

Italian

IN Calabria there lived not long ago a poor woman of low estate who had an only son called Cesarino di Berni, a youth of great discretion, and one endowed more richly with the gifts of nature than with those of fortune. It chanced on a certain day that Cesarino left his home and went into the country, and, having come into a deep and thick-leaved forest, he made his way into the midst of it, enchanted by the verdant beauty of the place. As he went on, he came upon a rocky cavern, in which he found in one place a litter of lion cubs, in another a litter of bear cubs, and in another a litter of wolf cubs, and, having taken one each of these, he carried them home with him, and with the greatest care and diligence brought them up together. The animals in course of time came to be so much attached one to another that they could not bear to be apart, and, besides this, they had become so tame and gentle with the people of the house that they hurt nobody. But, seeing that they were by nature wild animals, and only domesticated by chance, and that they had now attained the full strength of maturity, Cesarino would often take them with him to follow the chase, and would always come back laden with the spoil of the woods and rejoicing at his good luck. Thus by his hunting Cesarino supported both his old mother and himself, and after a time the old woman, marvelling at the great quantity of game which her son always brought home with him, asked him by what means he contrived to entrap so fine a spoil, whereupon Cesarino answered that he got his game by the help of the animals which she must often have seen about the house. At the same time he begged *Italian* her to be careful not to let this secret be known to any one, lest the animals should be taken away from them.

Before many days had passed it happened that the old mother forgathered with a neighbour of hers whom she held very dear, not merely because she was a worthy upright woman, but because she was kindly and obliging as well. And as they were talking of this thing and that, the neighbour said : " Neighbour, how is it that your son manages to take such great quantities of game ? " And in answer thereto the old woman, forgetful of her son's warning, told her all she asked, and, having taken leave of her, went back to her home.

Scarcely had the old mother parted from her neighbour when the husband of the latter came in, whereupon the wife went to meet him with a joyful face, and told him all the news she had just heard from her old neighbour. The husband, when he had learned how the matter stood, went straightway to find Cesarino, and, having fallen in with him, thus addressed him : " How is it, my son, that you go so often a-hunting, and never offer to take a comrade with you ? Such behaviour is hardly in agreement with the friendship which has always subsisted between us." Cesa-rino, when he heard these words, smiled somewhat, but made no answer to them, and on the morrow, without saying a word of farewell to his old mother or to his well-beloved sisters, he left his home, taking with him his three animals, and went out into the world to seek his fortune.

After he had travelled a very long distance, he came into Sicily, and there he found himself one day in a solitary uninhabited spot in the midst of which stood a hermitage, which he approached, and, after having entered it and found it void, he and his three animals bestowed themselves to rest therein. He had not been there very long when the hermit to whom the place belonged came back, and when

Italian he entered the door and saw the animals lying there, he was overcome with terror and turned to fly. But Cesarino, who had watched the hermit's approach, cried out : " My father, be not afraid, but come into your cell without fear, because all these animals you see are so tame and gentle that they will in no way do you any hurt." Whereupon the hermit, assured by these words of Cesarino, went into his humble cell. Now Cesarino was much worn out by the length of his journeying, and, turning to the hermit, he said : " My father, have you here by chance a morsel of bread and a drop of wine you can give me to bring back a little of my strength ? " " Assuredly I have, my son," replied the hermit, " but not perhaps of quality so good as you may desire." Then the hermit, when he had flayed and cut up some of the game he had brought with him, put it upon a spit to roast, and, having got ready the table and spread it with such poor viands as were at hand, he and Cesarino took their supper merrily together.

When they had finished their meal, the hermit said to Cesarino : " Not far from this place there lives a dragon whose poisonous breath destroys and annihilates everything around, nor is there found any one in the country who can withstand him, and so great is the ruin he works that before long all the peasants of the land will be forced to abandon their fields and fly elsewhere. And, over and beside this, it is necessary to send him every day the body of some human being to devour, for, failing this, he would destroy everything far and near. By a cruel and evil fate the one chosen by lot for to-morrow is the daughter of the king, who in beauty and worth and goodness excels every other maiden now alive, nor is there aught to be found in her which is not worthy of the highest praise. Of a truth, it is a foul mischance that so fair and virtuous a damsel should thus cruelly perish, and she herself all the while free of any offence."

68

CESARINO AND THE DRAGON

Cesarino, when he had listened to these words of the *Italian* hermit, thus replied : " Let not your courage fail you, holy father, and fear not that evil will befall us, for in a very short time you will see the maiden set free." And the next morning, almost before the first rays of dawn had appeared in the sky, Cesarino took his way to the spot where the dreadful monster had made his lair, taking along with him his three animals, and having come there, he beheld the daughter of the king, who had already been conveyed thither to be devoured by the beast. He went straightway towards her, and found her weeping bitterly, and comforted her with these words : " Weep not, lady, nor lament, for I am come hither to free you from your peril." But even as he spake, behold ! the ravenous dragon came forth with a mighty rush from its lair, and with its jaws open wide made ready to tear in pieces and devour the delicate body of the beautiful maiden, who, smitten with fear, trembled in every limb. Then Cesarino, stirred by pity for the damsel, took courage and urged on the three animals to attack the fierce and famished monster before them, and so valiantly did they grapple with him that they bore him to the ground and slew him. Whereupon Cesarino, taking a naked knife in his hand, cut out the tongue from the throat of the dragon and put it carefully in a bag ; then, without speaking a word to the damsel whom he had delivered from this horrible death, he took his leave and went back to the hermitage, and gave the holy father an account of the deed he had wrought. The hermit, when he understood that the dragon was indeed destroyed, and the young maiden set at liberty, and the country delivered from the horrible scourge which had lately vexed it, was wellnigh overcome with joy.

Now it happened that a certain peasant, a coarse, worthless rogue of a fellow, was passing by the spot where lay stretched out the dead body of the fierce and horrible monster, and as soon as he caught sight of the savage, fearsome beast he took in his hand the knife which he carried at his side, and struck off therewith the dragon's head from the body, and having placed the same in a large bag which he had with him, he took his way towards the city. As he went along the road at a rapid pace, he overtook the princess, who was going back to the king her father, and, having joined company with her, he went with her as far as the royal palace and led her into the presence of the king, who, as soon as he saw his daughter come back safe and sound, almost died from excess of gladness. Then the peasant, with a joyful air, took off the hat he wore on his head and thus addressed the king : " Sire, I claim by right this fair daughter of yours as my wife, seeing that I have delivered her from death." And having thus spoken the peasant, as a testimony of his word, drew forth from his bag the horrible head of the slain monster and laid it before the king. The king, when he beheld the head of the beast, once so fierce but now a thing of nought, and considered in his mind how his daughter had been rescued from death, and his country freed from the ravages of the dragon, gave orders for universal rejoicings, and for the preparation of a sumptuous feast, to which should be bidden all the ladies of the city. And a great crowd of these, splendidly attired, came to offer to the princess their good wishes for her delivery from death.

It happened that at this very same time, when they were getting ready all these feasts and rejoicings, the old hermit went into the city, where the news soon came to his ears how a certain peasant had slain the dragon, and how as a reward for his deed and for the liberation of the king's daughter, he was to have the damsel to wife. When the hermit heard this he was heavily grieved, and, putting aside for the time all thought of seeking for alms, he returned forthwith to his hermitage and made known to Cesarino the thing he had just heard. The youth, when he listened

70

to this, was much grieved, and having brought forth the *Italian* tongue of the slain dragon, he exhibited it to the hermit as a trustworthy proof that he had himself destroyed the wild beast. When the hermit had heard his story, and was fully persuaded that Cesarino was the slayer of the dragon, he betook himself to the presence of the king, and having withdrawn his ragged cowl from his head, he thus spake : " Most sacred majesty, it would in any case be a shameful thing if a malignant rascally fellow, one for whom a hole in the ground is a home good enough, should become the husband of a maiden who is the very flower of loveliness, the example of good manners, the mirror of courtesy, and richly dowered with every virtue ; but it becomes much worse when such a rogue seeks to win this prize by deceiving your majesty, and by declaring the lies which issue from his throat to be the truth. Now I, who am very jealous of your majesty's honour, and eager to be of service to the princess your daughter, am come here to make it manifest to you that he who goes about making boast of having delivered your daughter is not the man who slew the dragon. Wherefore, O most sacred majesty, keep open your eyes, and your ears likewise, and listen to one who has your welfare at heart."

The king, when he heard the bold utterances of the hermit, was fully assured that the old man's words were those of faithful and devoted love, and gave heed to them forthwith. He issued orders at once that all the feasts and rejoicings should be countermanded, and directed the hermit to tell him the name of the man who was the true rescuer of his daughter. The hermit, who wished for nothing better, said : " Sire, there is no need to make any mystery about his name ; but if it will fall in with your majesty's wishes, I will bring him here into your presence, and you will see a youth of fair aspect, graceful, seemly, and lovable, gifted with manners so noble and honest that I have never yet met

71

Italian another to equal him." The king, who was already greatly taken with this picture of the young man, bade the hermit bring him into his presence straightway. The hermit, having gone out of the king's palace, returned to his cabin and told Cesarino what he had done.

The youth, after he had taken the dragon's tongue and put it in a wallet, went, accompanied by the hermit and the three animals, to the king's presence, and kneeling reverently on his knees, spake thus : " Most sacred majesty, the fatigue and the labour were indeed mine, but the honour belongs to others. I and these three animals of mine slew the wild beast in order to set your daughter at liberty." Then the king said : " What proof can you give me that you really slew this beast, inasmuch as this other man has brought to me the head thereof, which you see suspended here ? " Cesarino answered : " I do not ask you to take the word of your daughter, which would assuredly be an all-sufficient testimony. I will simply offer to you one token, of a nature no one can gainsay, that I and no other was the slayer of the beast. Examine well the head you have in your keeping, and you will find that the tongue is lacking thereto." Whereupon the king caused the dragon's head to be examined, and found it without a tongue ; so Cesarino, having put his hand in his bag, drew forth the tongue of the dragon, which was of enormous size—so great a one had never before been seen—and showed clearly thereby that he had slain the savage beast. The king, after having heard confirmation from his daughter, and on account of this production of the tongue by Cesarino, and divers other proofs which were offered, commanded them at once to take the villainous peasant and to strike off his head from his body. Then with great feasts and rejoicings the nuptials of Cesarino and the princess were celebrated.

When the news was brought to the mother and the sisters of Cesarino that he had slain the wild beast and had rescued

the princess, and that moreover the damsel had been given *Italian*
him to wife, they resolved to travel to Sicily, and, having
taken passage in a ship, they were quickly borne thither
before a favourable wind, and met with a very honourable
reception.   But these women had not been long in the
land before they grew so envious of Cesarino's good fortune
that they took thought of nothing else than how they might
work his downfall, and their hatred, which increased day
by day, at last stirred them to cause him to be privily
murdered.   Then, having considered in their minds divers
deadly stratagems, they determined at last to take a bone
and to sharpen the point thereof, then to dip the same in
venom, and to place it in Cesarino's bed with the point
upwards, so that when he should go to rest and throw
himself down on the bed, as is the wont of young people,
he should give himself a poisonous wound.   Having thus
determined, they set to work to carry out their wicked
design forthwith.   One day, when the hour for retiring to
rest had come, Cesarino went with his wife into the bed-
chamber.   And having thrown off all his clothes and his
shirt, he lay down on the bed and struck his left side against
the sharp point of the bone.   And so severe was the wound
that his body forthwith swelled on account of the poison,
and when this reached his heart he died.   His wife, when
she saw that her husband was dead, began to cry aloud and
to weep bitterly, and the courtiers, attracted by the noise,
ran to the chamber, where they found Cesarino dead.   Having
turned the corpse over and over again, they found it inflated
and black as a raven, and on this account they suspected
that he had been killed by poison.   When the king heard
what had occurred, he caused the strictest inquisition to
be made ; but, having come upon no clue, he gave over the
search, and, together with his daughter and the whole
court, put on the deepest mourning, and ordered the body
of Cesarino to be buried with the most solemn funeral rites.

Italian   While these stately obsequies were being carried out, the mother and sisters of Cesarino began to be sore afraid lest the lion and the bear and the wolf (when they should find out that their master was dead) might scent out the treachery that had been used against him ; so, having taken counsel one with another, they hit upon the plan of sealing up the ears of the three animals, and they managed to carry out their design. But they did not seal up the ears of the wolf so close but that he was able to hear a little with one of them as to what had been going on. So, after the dead body had been taken to the sepulchre, the wolf said to the lion and the bear : " Comrades, it seems to me that there is bad news about." But these two, whose ears were completely stopped, could not hear what he said, and when he repeated the same words they understood him no better. But the wolf went on making signs and gestures to them, so that at last they knew what he wanted to tell them, namely, that some one was dead. Then the bear set to work with his hard crooked claws, and dug down into the lion's ears, deep enough to bring out the seal. And the lion did the same to the bear and the wolf.

As soon as they had all got back their hearing, the wolf said to his companions : " It seems to me as if I had heard men talking of our master's death." And seeing that their master came not, as was his wont, to visit them and to give them their food, they held it for certain that he must be dead. Whereupon they all left the house together, and came straight to the spot where the dead body was being borne to the grave. As soon as the priests and the others who were assisting at the funeral saw the three animals, they all took to flight, and the men who were bearing the corpse put it down and fled likewise, but some there were of firmer courage who wished to see the end of the affair. Immediately the animals began to work hard with their teeth and claws, and before long they had stripped the grave-

So valiantly did they grapple with him that
they bore him to the ground and slew him

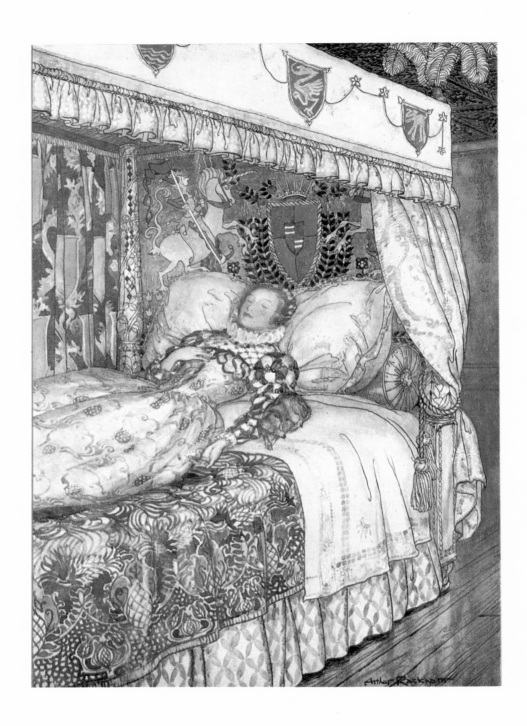

The Sleeping Princess

clothes off their master's body, and, having examined it *Italian* very closely, found the fatal wound. Then the lion said to the bear : " Brother, now is the time that we want a little of that grease which you carry in your inside ; for if we shall be able to anoint our master's wound therewith, he will straightway recover." Then answered the bear : " No need to say another word. I will open my mouth as wide as I possibly can ; then you may put your paw down my throat, and bring up as much grease as you will want." So the lion put his paw down the bear's throat—the bear drawing himself together the while, so that he might be able to thrust it deep down—and when he had extracted all the grease he wanted, he anointed his master's wound therewith on all sides, and within and without. When the wound had become somewhat softened he sucked it with his mouth, and then thrust into it a certain herb the virtue of which was so potent that it immediately began to work upon the heart, and in a very short time rekindled its fire. Then Cesarino little by little recovered his strength and was brought back to life.

When those who were standing by saw this marvel they were struck with amazement, and straightway ran to the king to tell him that Cesarino was restored to life. The king, when he heard these tidings, went to meet him, accompanied by his daughter, whose name was Dorothea, and they embraced him and kissed him in the joy they felt over this unexpected ending of the affair, and with gladsome rejoicing led him back to the king's palace.

The news of Cesarino's resurrection soon came to the ears of his mother and sisters and disturbed them mightily ; nevertheless, feigning to be overjoyed thereat, they repaired to the palace to felicitate him with the rest ; but, as soon as they came into Cesarino's presence, his wound immediately threw out a great quantity of blood. On seeing this they were struck with confusion, and their faces turned pale,

75

Italian whereupon the king, growing suspicious of their guilt, bade his guards seize them and put them to the torture. Which, having been done, they confessed all ; so the king forthwith commanded them to be burned alive, and Cesarino and Dorothea lived long and happily together, and left children to rule in their stead. The three animals, until they died in the course of nature, were tended with the utmost care and affection.

WHAT CAME OF PICKING FLOWERS

THERE was once a woman who had three daughters *Portuguese* whom she loved very much. One day the eldest was walking in a water-meadow, when she saw a pink growing in the stream. She stooped to pick the flower, but her hand had scarcely touched it when she vanished altogether. The next morning the second sister went out into the meadow to see if she could find any traces of the lost girl, and as a branch of lovely roses lay trailing across her path, she bent down to move it away, and in so doing could not resist plucking one of the roses. In a moment she too had disappeared. Wondering what could have become of her two sisters, the youngest followed in their footsteps and fell a victim to a branch of delicious white

Portuguese jasmine. So the old woman was left without any daughters at all.

She wept, and wept, and wept, all day and all night, and went on weeping so long that her son, who had been a little boy when his sisters disappeared, grew up to be a tall youth. Then one night he asked his mother to tell him what was the matter.

When he had heard the whole story he said : " Give me your blessing, mother, and I will go and search the world till I find them."

So he set forth, and after he had travelled several miles without any adventures, he came upon three big boys fighting in the road. He stopped and inquired what they were fighting about, and one of them answered :

" My lord ! our father left to us, when he died, a pair of boots, a key, and a cap. Whoever puts on the boots and wishes himself in any place will find himself there ; the key will open every door in the world ; and with the cap on your head no one can see you.   Now our eldest brother wants to have all three things for himself, and we wish to draw lots for them."

" Oh, that is easily settled," said the youth.   " I will throw this stone as far as I can, and the one who picks it up first shall have the three things."   So he took the stone and flung it, and while the three brothers were running after it, he hastily drew on the boots, and said : " Boots, take me to the place where I shall find my eldest sister."

The next moment the young man was standing on a steep mountain before the gates of a strong castle guarded by bolts and bars and iron chains. The key, which he had not forgotten to put in his pocket, opened the doors one by one, and he walked through a number of halls and corridors, till he met a beautiful and richly dressed young lady who started back in surprise at the sight of him, and

78

exclaimed : " Oh, sir, how did you contrive to get in here ? " *Portuguese*
The young man replied that he was her brother, and told
her by what means he had been able to pass through the
doors.   In return, she told him how happy she was, except
for one thing, and that was, her husband lay under a spell,
and could never break it till there should be put to death
a man who could not die.

They talked together for a long time, and then the lady
said he had better leave her as she expected her husband
back at any moment, and he might not like him to be there ;
but the young man assured her she need not be afraid, as
he had with him a cap which would make him invisible.
They were still deep in conversation when the door suddenly
opened, and a bird flew in, but he saw nothing unusual, for,
at the first noise, the youth had put on his cap.   The lady
jumped up and brought a large golden basin, into which
the bird flew, reappearing directly after as a handsome
man.   Turning to his wife, he cried : " I am sure some one
is in the room ! "   She got frightened, and declared that
she was quite alone, but her husband persisted, and in the
end she had to confess the truth.

" But if he is really your brother, why did you hide him ? "
asked he.   " I believe you are telling me a lie, and if he
comes back I shall kill him ! "

At this the youth took off his cap, and came forward.
Then the husband saw that he was indeed so like his wife
that he doubted her word no longer, and embraced his
brother-in-law with delight.   Drawing a feather from his
bird's skin, he said : " If you are in danger and cry, ' Come
and help me, King of the Birds,' everything will go well
with you."

The young man thanked him and went away, and after
he had left the castle he told the boots that they must take
him to the place where his second sister was living.   As
before, he found himself at the gates of a huge castle, and

Portuguese within was his second sister, very happy with her husband, who loved her dearly, but longing for the moment when he should be set free from the spell that kept him half his life a fish. When he arrived and had been introduced by his wife to her brother, he welcomed him warmly, and gave him a fish-scale, saying : " If you are in danger, call to me, ' Come and help me, King of the Fishes,' and everything will go well with you."

The young man thanked him and took his leave, and when he was outside the gates he told the boots to take him to the place where his youngest sister lived. The boots carried him to a dark cavern, with steps of iron leading up to it. Inside she sat, weeping and sobbing, and as she had done nothing else the whole time she had been there the poor girl had grown very thin. When she saw a man standing before her, she sprang to her feet and exclaimed : " Oh, whoever you are, save me and take me from this horrible place ! " Then he told her who he was, and how he had seen her sisters, whose happiness was spoilt by the spell under which both their husbands lay, and she, in turn, related her story. She had been carried off in the water-meadow by a horrible monster, who wanted to make her marry him by force, and had kept her a prisoner all these years because she would not submit to his will. Every day he came to beg her to consent to his wishes, and to remind her that there was no hope of her being set free, as he was the most constant man in the world, and besides that he could never die. At these words the youth remembered his two enchanted brothers-in-law, and he advised his sister to promise to marry the old man, if he would tell her why he could never die. Suddenly everything began to tremble, as if it was shaken by a whirlwind, and the old man entered, and flinging himself at the feet of the girl, he said : " Are you still determined never to marry me ? If so you will have to sit there weeping till the

80

end of the world, for I shall always be faithful to my *Portuguese* wish to marry you ! " "Well, I will marry you," she said, "if you will tell me why it is that you can never die."

Then the old man burst into peals of laughter. "Ah, ah, ah ! You are thinking how you would be able to kill me ? Well, to do that you would have to find an iron casket which lies at the bottom of the sea, and has a white dove inside, and then you would have to find the egg which the dove laid, and bring it here, and dash it against my head." And he laughed again in his certainty that no one had ever got down to the bottom of the sea, and that if they did, they would never find the casket, or be able to open it. When he could speak once more, he said : " Now you will be obliged to marry me, as you know my secret." But she begged so hard that the wedding might be put off for three days that he consented, and went away rejoicing at his victory. When he had disappeared, the brother took off the cap which had kept him invisible all this time, and told his sister not to lose heart as he hoped in three days she would be free. Then he drew on his boots, and wished himself at the sea-shore, and there he was directly. Drawing out the fish-scale, he cried : " Come and help me, King of the Fishes ! " and his brother-in-law swam up, and asked what he could do. The young man related the story, and when he had finished his listener summoned all the fishes to his presence. The last to arrive was a little sardine, who apologized for being so late, but said she had hurt herself by knocking her head against an iron casket that lay at the bottom of the sea. The king ordered several of the largest and strongest of his subjects to take the little sardine as a guide, and bring him the iron casket. They soon returned with the box placed across their backs and laid it down before him. Then the youth produced the key and said, " Key, open that box ! " and the key opened it, and though they were all

81

Portuguese crowding round, ready to catch it, the white dove within flew away.

It was useless to go after it, and for a moment the young man's heart sank. The next minute, however, he remembered that he had still his feather, and drew it out crying, " Come to me, King of the Birds ! " and a rushing noise was heard, and the King of the Birds perched on his shoulder, and asked what he could do to help him. His brother-in-law told him the whole story, and when he had finished the King of the Birds commanded all his subjects to hasten to his presence. In an instant the air was dark with birds of all sizes, and at the very last came the white dove, apologizing for being so late by saying that an old friend had arrived at his nest, and he had been obliged to give him some dinner. The King of the Birds ordered some of them to show the young man the white dove's nest, and when they reached it, there lay the egg which was to break the spell and set them all free. When it was safely in his pocket, he told the boots to carry him straight to the cavern where his youngest sister sat awaiting him.

Now it was already far on into the third day, which the old man had fixed for the wedding, and when the youth reached the cavern with his cap on his head, he found the monster there, urging the girl to keep her word and let the marriage take place at once. At a sign from her brother she sat down and invited the old monster to lay his head on her lap. He did so with delight, and her brother standing behind her back passed her the egg unseen. She took it, and dashed it straight at the horrible head, and the monster started, and with a groan that people took for the rumblings of an earthquake, he turned over and died.

As the breath went out of his body the husbands of the two eldest daughters resumed their proper shapes, and,

82

sending for their mother-in-law, whose sorrow was so *Portuguese* unexpectedly turned into joy, they had a great feast, and the youngest sister was rich to the end of her days with the treasures she found in the cave, collected by the monster.

THE ADVENTURES OF LITTLE PEACHLING

Japanese MANY hundred years ago there lived an honest old woodcutter and his wife. One fine morning the old man went off to the hills with his billhook, to gather a faggot of sticks, while his wife went down to the river to wash the dirty clothes. When she came to the river she saw a peach floating down the stream ; so she picked it up, and carried it home with her, thinking to give it to her husband to eat when he should come in. The old man soon came down from the hills, and the good wife set the peach before him, when, just as she was inviting him to eat it, the fruit split in two, and a little puling baby was born into the world. So the old couple took the babe, and brought it up as their own ; and because it had been born in a peach, they called it " Momotaro," or Little Peachling, for " Momo " means a peach, and " Taro " is the termination of the names of eldest sons.

By degrees Little Peachling grew up to be strong and brave, and at last one day he said to his old foster-parents :

84

LITTLE PEACHLING

"I am going to the ogres' island to carry off the riches *Japanese* that they have stored up there. Pray, then, make me some millet dumplings for my journey."

So the old folk ground the millet, and made the dumplings for him; and Little Peachling, after taking an affectionate leave of them, cheerfully set out on his travels.

As he was journeying on, he fell in with an ape, who gibbered at him, and said : " Kia ! kia ! kia ! where are you off to, Little Peachling ? "

"I'm going to the ogres' island, to carry off their treasure," answered Little Peachling.

" What are you carrying at your girdle ? "

" I'm carrying the very best millet dumplings in all Japan."

" If you'll give me one, I will go with you," said the ape.

So Little Peachling gave one of his dumplings to the ape, who received it and followed him. When he had gone a little farther he heard a pheasant calling :

" Ken ! ken ! ken ! where are you off to, Master Peach-ling ? "

Little Peachling answered as before; and the pheasant, having begged and obtained a millet dumpling, entered his service, and followed him. A little while after this they met a dog, who cried :

" Bow ! wow ! wow ! whither away, Master Peachling ? "

" I'm going off to the ogres' island, to carry off their treasure."

" If you will give me one of those nice millet dumplings of yours, I will go with you," said the dog.

" With all my heart," said Little Peachling. So he went on his way, with the ape, the pheasant, and the dog following after him.

When they got to the ogres' island, the pheasant flew over the castle gate, and the ape clambered over the castle wall, while Little Peachling, leading the dog, forced in the gate,

Japanese and got into the castle. Then they did battle with the ogres, and put them to flight, and took their king prisoner. So all the ogres did homage to Little Peachling, and brought out the treasures which they had laid up. There were caps and coats that made their wearers invisible, jewels which governed the ebb and flow of the tide, coral, musk, emeralds, amber, and tortoise-shell, besides gold and silver. All these were laid before Little Peachling by the conquered ogres.

So Little Peachling went home laden with riches, and maintained his foster-parents in peace and plenty for the remainder of their lives.

THE FOX'S WEDDING

ONCE upon a time there was a young white fox, whose Japanese name was Fukuyémon. When he had reached the fitting age he shaved off his forelock and began to think of taking to himself a beautiful bride. The old fox, his father, resolved to give up his inheritance to his son, and retired into private life ; so the young fox, in gratitude for this, laboured hard and earnestly to increase his patrimony. Now it happened that in a famous old family of foxes there was a beautiful young lady-fox, with such lovely fur that the fame of her jewel-like charms was spread far and wide. The young white fox, who had heard of this, was bent on making her his wife, and a meeting was arranged between them. There was not a fault to be found on either side ; so the preliminaries were settled, and the wedding presents sent from the bridegroom to the bride's house, with congratulatory speeches from the messenger, which were duly acknowledged by the person deputed to receive the gifts ; the bearers, of course, received the customary fee in copper cash.

When the ceremonies had been concluded, an auspicious day was chosen for the bride to go to her husband's house, and she was carried off in solemn procession during a shower of rain, the sun shining all the while. In Japan a shower during sunshine is called " The fox's bride going to her husband's house." After the ceremonies of drinking wine had been gone through, the bride changed her dress, and the wedding was concluded, without let or hindrance, amid singing and dancing and merry-making.

The bride and bridegroom lived lovingly together, and a litter of little foxes was born to them, to the great joy of the old grandsire, who treated the little cubs as tenderly as if they had been butterflies or flowers. " They're the

87

Japanese very image of their old grandfather," said he, as proud as possible. "As for medicine, bless them, they're so healthy that they'll never need a copper coin's worth!"

As soon as they were old enough they were carried off to the temple of Inari Sama, the patron saint of foxes, and the old grandparents prayed that they might be delivered from dogs and all the other ills to which fox flesh is heir.

In this way the white fox by degrees waxed old and prosperous, and his children, year by year, became more and more numerous around him; so that, happy in his family and his business, every recurring spring brought him fresh cause for joy.

THE TONGUE-CUT SPARROW

ONCE upon a time there lived an old man and an old *Japanese* woman. The old man, who had a kind heart, kept a young sparrow, which he tenderly nurtured. But the dame was a cross-grained old thing ; and one day, when the sparrow had pecked at some paste with which she was going to starch her linen, she flew into a great rage, and cut the sparrow's tongue and let it loose. When the old man came home from the hills and found that the bird had flown, he asked what had become of it ; so the old woman answered that she had cut its tongue and let it go, because it had stolen her starching-paste. Now the old man, hearing this cruel tale, was sorely grieved, and thought to himself : "Alas ! where can my bird be gone ? Poor thing ! Poor little tongue-cut sparrow ! where is your home now ? " and he wandered far and wide, seeking for his pet, and crying : " Mr. Sparrow ! Mr. Sparrow ! where are you living ? "

One day, at the foot of a certain mountain, the old man fell in with the lost bird ; and when they had congratulated one another on their mutual safety, the sparrow led the old man to his home, and, having introduced him to his wife and chicks, set before him all sorts of dainties, and entertained him hospitably.

"Please partake of our humble fare," said the sparrow. "Poor as it is, you are very welcome."

Its wife and children and grandchildren all served at table, and when the guest could drink no more, the sparrow threw down the drinking-cup, and danced a jig in his honour.

"What a polite sparrow ! " answered the old man, who remained for a long time as the sparrow's guest, and was daily feasted right royally. At last the old man said that

Japanese he must take his leave and return home ; and the bird, bringing out two wicker baskets, begged him to carry them with him as a parting present. One of the baskets was heavy, and the other was light ; so the old man, saying that as he was feeble and stricken in years he would only accept the light one, shouldered it, and trudged off home, leaving the sparrow family disconsolate at parting from him.

When the old man got home the dame grew very angry, and began to scold him, saying : " Well, and pray where have you been this many a day ? A pretty thing, indeed, to be gadding about at your time of life ! "

" Oh ! " replied he, " I have been on a visit to the sparrows ; and when I came away, they gave me this wicker basket as a parting gift." Then they opened the basket to see what was inside, and, lo and behold ! it was full of gold and silver and jewels and rolls of silk. When the old woman, who was as greedy as she was cross, saw all the riches displayed before her, she changed her scolding strain, and could not contain herself for joy.

" I'll go and call upon the sparrows too," said she, " and get a pretty present." So she asked the old man the way to the sparrows' house, and set forth on her journey. Following his directions, she at last met the tongue-cut sparrow, and exclaimed :

" Well met ! well met ! Mr. Sparrow. I have been looking forward to the pleasure of seeing you." So she tried to flatter and cajole the sparrow by soft speeches.

The bird could not but invite the dame to its home ; but it took no pains to feast her, and said nothing about a parting gift. She, however, was not to be put off ; so she asked for something to carry away with her in remembrance of her visit. The sparrow accordingly produced two baskets, as before, and the greedy old woman, choosing the heavier of the two, carried it off with her. But when she opened

90

Thyl Ulenspiegel and the Seven

*The birds show the young man the white
dove's nest*

THE TONGUE-CUT SPARROW

the basket to see what was inside, all sorts of hob- *Japanese*
goblins and devils sprang out of it, and began to torment
her.

But the old man adopted a son, and his family grew rich
and prosperous. What a happy old man !

FROST

Russian **T**HERE was an old man who had a wife and three
daughters. The wife had no love for the eldest of
the three, who was her stepdaughter, but was
always scolding her. Moreover, she used to make her get
up ever so early in the morning, and gave her all the work
of the house to do. Before daybreak the girl would feed
the cattle and give them to drink, fetch wood and water
indoors, light the fire in the stove, give the room a wash,
mend the dresses, and set everything in order. Even then
her stepmother was never satisfied, but would grumble
away at Marfa, exclaiming :

"What a lazybones ! what a slut ! Why here's a brush

not in its place, and there's something put wrong, and *Russian* she's left the muck inside the house ! "

The girl held her peace, and wept ; she tried in every way to accommodate herself to her stepmother, and to be of service to her stepsisters. But they, taking pattern by their mother, were always insulting Marfa, quarrelling with her, and making her cry ; that was even a pleasure to them ! As for them, they lay in bed late, washed themselves in water got ready for them, dried themselves with a clean towel, and didn't sit down to work till after dinner.

Well, our girls grew and grew, until they grew up and were old enough to be married. The old man felt sorry for his eldest daughter, whom he loved because she was industrious and obedient, never was obstinate, always did as she was bid, and never uttered a word of contradiction. But he didn't know how he was to help her in her trouble. He was feeble, his wife was a scold, and her daughters were as obstinate as they were indolent.

Well, the old folk set to work to consider—the husband how he could get his daughters settled, the wife how she could get rid of the eldest one. One day she says to him :

" I say, old man ! let's get Marfa married."

" Gladly," says he, slinking off to the sleeping-place above the stove. But his wife called after him :

" Get up early to-morrow, old man, harness the mare to the sledge, and drive away with Marfa. And, Marfa, get your things together in a basket, and put on a clean shift ; you're going away to-morrow on a visit."

Poor Marfa was delighted to hear of such a piece of good luck as being invited on a visit, and she slept comfortably all night. Early next morning she got up, washed herself, prayed to God, got all her things together, packed them away in proper order, dressed herself in her best things, and looked something like a lass—a bride fit for any place whatsoever !

93

Russian   Now it was winter-time, and out of doors was a rattling frost. Early in the morning, between daybreak and sunrise, the old man harnessed the mare to the sledge, and led it up to the steps. Then he went indoors, sat down on the window-sill, and said :

" Now then, I've got everything ready."

" Sit down to table and swallow your victuals ! " replied the old woman.

The old man sat down to table, and made his daughter sit by his side. On the table stood a pannier ; he took out a loaf, and cut bread for himself and his daughter. Meantime his wife served up a dish of old cabbage soup, and said :

" There, my pigeon, eat and be off ; I've looked at you quite enough ! Drive Marfa to her bridegroom, old man. And look here, old greybeard, drive straight along the road at first, and then turn off from the road to the right, you know, into the forest—right up to the big pine that stands on the hill, and there hand Marfa over to Frost."

The old man opened his eyes wide, also his mouth, and stopped eating, and the girl began lamenting.

" Now then, what are you hanging your chaps and squealing about ? " said her stepmother. " Surely your bridegroom is a beauty, and he's that rich ! Why, just see what a lot of things belong to him : the firs, the pine-tops, and the birches, all in their robes of down—ways and means that any one might envy ; and he himself a bogatir, a hero of romance ! "

The old man silently placed the things on the sledge, made his daughter put on a warm pelisse, and set off on the journey. After a time he reached the forest, turned off from the road, and drove across the frozen snow. When he got into the depths of the forest he stopped, made his daughter get out, laid her basket under the tall pine, and said :

" Sit here, and await the bridegroom. And mind you *Russian* receive him as pleasantly as you can."

Then he turned his horse round and drove off homewards.

The girl sat and shivered. The cold had pierced her through. She would fain have cried aloud, but she had not strength enough ; only her teeth chattered. Suddenly she heard a sound. Not far off, Frost was cracking away on a fir. From fir to fir was he leaping, and snapping his fingers. Presently he appeared on that very pine under which the maiden was sitting, and from above her head he cried :

" Art thou warm, maiden ? "

" Warm, warm am I, dear Father Frost," she replied.

Frost began to descend lower, all the more cracking and snapping his fingers. To the maiden said Frost :

" Art thou warm, maiden ? Art thou warm, fair one ? "

The girl could scarcely draw her breath, but still she replied : " Warm am I, Frost dear ; warm am I, father dear ! "

Frost began cracking more than ever, and more loudly did he snap his fingers, and to the maiden he said :

" Art thou warm, maiden ? Art thou warm, pretty one ? Art thou warm, my darling ? "

The girl was by this time numb with cold, and she could scarcely make herself heard as she replied :

" Oh ! quite warm, Frost dearest ! "

Then Frost took pity on the girl, wrapped her up in furs, and warmed her with blankets.

Next morning the old woman said to her husband :

" Drive out, old greybeard, and wake the young couple ! "

The old man harnessed his horse and drove off. When he came to where his daughter was, he found she was alive and had got a good pelisse, a costly bridal veil, and a pannier with rich gifts. He stowed everything away on the sledge

Russian without saying a word, took his seat on it with his daughter, and drove back. They reached home, and the daughter fell at her stepmother's feet. The old woman was thunder-struck when she saw the girl alive, and the new pelisse and the basket of linen.

"Ah, you wretch!" she cries. "But you shan't trick me!"

Well, a little later the old woman says to her husband:

"Take my daughters, too, to their bridegroom. The presents he's made are nothing to what he'll give them."

Well, early next morning the old woman gave her girls their breakfast, dressed them as befitted brides, and sent them off on their journey. In the same way as before the old man left the girls under the pine.

There the girls sat, and kept laughing and saying:

"Whatever is mother thinking of? All of a sudden to marry both of us off! As if there were no lads in our village, forsooth! Some rubbishy fellow may come, and goodness knows who he may be!"

The girls were wrapped up in pelisses, but for all that they felt the cold.

"I say, Prascovia, the frost's skinning me alive! Well, if our bridegroom doesn't come quick, we shall be frozen to death here!"

"Don't go talking nonsense, Mashka; as if suitors turned up in the forenoon! Why, it's hardly dinner-time yet!"

"But I say, Prascovia, if only one comes, which of us will he take?"

"Not you, you stupid goose!"

"Then it will be you, I suppose!"

"Of course it will be me!"

"You, indeed! There now, have done talking stuff and treating people like fools!"

96

FROST

Meanwhile Frost had numbed the girls' hands, so our *Russian* damsels folded them under their dress, and then went on quarrelling as before.

"What, you fright! you sleepy-face! you abominable shrew! Why, you don't know so much as how to begin weaving; and as to going on with it, you haven't an idea!"

"Aha, boaster! and what is it you know? Why, nothing at all except to go out to merry-makings and lick your lips there. We'll soon see which he'll take first!"

While the girls went on scolding like that, they began to freeze in downright earnest. Suddenly they both cried out at once:

"Why ever is he so long coming? Do you know, you've turned quite blue!"

Now, a good way off, Frost had begun cracking, snapping his fingers, and leaping from fir to fir. To the girls it sounded as if some one was coming.

"Listen, Prascovia! He's coming at last, and with bells too!"

"Get along with you! I won't listen; my skin is peeling with cold."

"And yet you're still expecting to get married!"

Then they began blowing on their fingers.

Nearer and nearer came Frost. At length he appeared on the pine, above the heads of the girls, and said to them:

"Are ye warm, maidens? Are ye warm, pretty ones? Are ye warm, my darlings?"

"Oh, Frost, it's awfully cold! We're utterly perished! We're expecting a bridegroom, but the confounded fellow has disappeared."

Frost slid lower down the tree, cracked away more, snapped his fingers oftener than before.

"Are ye warm, maidens? Are ye warm, pretty ones?"

Russian   " Get along with you ! Are you blind that you can't see our hands and feet are quite dead ? "

Still lower descended Frost, still more put forth his might, and said :

" Are ye warm, maidens ? "

" Into the bottomless pit with you ! Out of sight, accursed one ! " cried the girls—and became lifeless forms.

Next morning the old woman said to her husband :

" Old man, go and get the sledge harnessed ; put an armful of hay in it, and take some sheepskin wraps. I dare say the girls are half-dead with cold. There's a terrible frost outside ! And, mind you, old greybeard, do it quickly ! "

Before the old man could manage to get a bite he was out of doors and on his way. When he came to where his daughters were he found them dead. So he lifted the girls on to the sledge, wrapped a blanket round them, and covered them up with a bark mat. The old woman saw him from afar, ran out to meet him, and called out ever so loud :

" Where are the girls ? "

" In the sledge."

The old woman lifted the mat, undid the blanket, and found the girls both dead.

Then like a thunderstorm she broke out against her husband, abusing him, and saying :

" What have you done, you old wretch ? You have destroyed my daughters, the children of my own flesh and blood, my never-enough-to-be-gazed-on seedlings, my beautiful berries ! I will thrash you with the tongs ; I will give it you with the stove-rake."

" That's enough, you old goose ! You flattered yourself you were going to get riches, but your daughters were too stiff-necked. How was I to blame ? It was you yourself would have it."

98

FROST

The old woman was in a rage at first, and used bad lan- *Russian*
guage ; but afterwards she made it up with her stepdaughter,
and they all lived together peaceably, and thrived, and bore
no malice. A neighbour made an offer of marriage, the
wedding was celebrated, and Marfa is now living happily.
The old man frightens his grandchildren with stories about
Frost, and doesn't let them have their own way.

THE GOLDEN APPLE-TREE AND
THE NINE PEAHENS

Serbian ONCE upon a time there lived a king who had three sons. Now, before the king's palace grew a golden apple-tree, which in one and the same night blossomed, bore fruit, and lost all its fruit, though no one could tell who took the apples. One day the king, speaking to his eldest son, said : " I should like to know who takes the fruit from our apple-tree ! " And the son said : " I will keep guard to-night, and will see who gathers the apples." So when the evening came he went and laid himself down, under the apple-tree, upon the ground to watch. Just, however, as the apples ripened he fell asleep, and when he awoke in the morning there was not a single one left on the tree. Whereupon he went and told his father what had happened. Then the second son offered to keep watch by the tree, but he had no better success than his eldest brother.

So the turn came to the king's youngest son to keep guard. He made his preparations, brought his bed under the tree and immediately went to sleep. Before midnight he awoke and looked up at the tree and saw how the apples ripened, and how the whole palace was lit up by their shining. At that minute nine peahens flew towards the tree, and eight of them settled on its branches, but the ninth alighted near him and turned instantly into a beautiful girl—so beautiful, indeed, that the whole kingdom could not produce one who could in any way compare with her. She stayed, conversing kindly with him, till after midnight, then, thanking him for the golden apples, she prepared to depart ; but, as he begged she would leave him one, she gave him two, one for himself and one for the king his father. Then the girl turned again into a peahen, and flew away with the other eight. Next morning, the king's son took the two apples to his father,

100

and the king was much pleased, and praised his son. When the evening came, the king's youngest son took his place again under the apple-tree to keep guard over it. He again conversed as he had done the night before with the beautiful girl, and brought to his father, the next morning, two apples as before. But, after he had succeeded so well several nights, his two elder brothers grew envious because he had been able to do what they could not. At length they found an old woman, who promised to discover how the youngest brother had succeeded in saving the two apples. So, as the evening came, the old woman stole softly under the bed which stood under the apple-tree, and hid herself. And after a while came also the king's son, and laid himself down as usual to sleep. When it was near midnight the nine peahens flew up as before, and eight of them settled on the branches, and the ninth stood by his bed, and turned into a most beautiful girl.

Then the old woman slowly took hold of one of the girl's curls and cut it off, and the girl immediately rose up, changed again into a peahen, and flew away, and the other peahens followed her, and so they all disappeared. Then the king's son jumped up, and cried out, " What is that ? " and, looking under the bed, he saw the old woman, and drew her out. Next morning he ordered her to be tied to a horse's tail, and so torn to pieces. But the peahens never came back, so the king's son was very sad for a long time, and wept at his loss. At length he determined to go and look after his peahen ; resolving never to come back again unless he should find her. When he told the king his father of his intention, the king begged him not to go away, and told him that he would find him another beautiful girl, and that he might choose out of the whole kingdom.

But all the king's persuasions were useless, so his son went into the world, taking only one servant to serve him— to search everywhere for his peahen. After many travels

Serbian he came one day to a lake. Now by the lake stood a large and beautiful palace. In the palace lived an old woman as queen, and with the queen lived a girl, her daughter. He said to the old woman : " For heaven's sake, grandmother, do you know anything about nine golden peahens ? " And the old woman answered : " Oh, my son, I know all about them ; they come every midday to bathe in the lake. But what do you want with them ? Let them be, think nothing about them. Here is my daughter. Such a beautiful girl ! and such an heiress ! All my wealth will remain to you if you marry her." But he, burning with desire to see the peahens, would not listen to what the old woman spoke about her daughter.

Next morning, when day dawned, the prince prepared to go down to the lake to wait for the peahens. Then the old queen bribed the servant and gave him a little pair of bellows, and said : " Do you see these bellows ? When you come to the lake you must blow secretly with them behind his neck, and then he will fall asleep, and not be able to speak to the peahens." The mischievous servant did as the old woman told him ; when he went with his master down to the lake, he took occasion to blow with the bellows behind his neck, and the poor prince fell asleep just as though he were dead. Shortly after, the nine peahens came flying, and eight of them alighted by the lake, but the ninth flew towards him as he sat on horseback and caressed him, and tried to awaken him. "Awake, my darling ! Awake, my heart ! Awake, my soul ! " But for all that he knew nothing, just as if he were dead. After they had bathed, all the peahens flew away together, and after they were gone the prince woke up, and said to his servant : " What has happened ? Did they not come ? " The servant told him they had been there, and that eight of them had bathed, but the ninth had sat by him on his horse, and caressed and tried to awaken him. Then the king's son was so angry that he
102

almost killed himself in his rage. Next morning, he went *Serbian*
down again to the shore to wait for the peahens, and rode
about a long time till the servant again found an opportunity
of blowing the bellows behind his neck, so that he again fell
asleep as though dead. Hardly had he fallen asleep before
the nine peahens came flying, and eight of them alighted
by the water, but the ninth settled down by the side of his
horse and caressed him, and cried out to awaken him :
" Arise, my darling ! Arise, my heart ! Arise, my soul ! "

But it was of no use ; the prince slept on as if he were
dead. Then she said to the servant : " Tell your master
to-morrow he can see us here again, but nevermore."
With these words the peahens flew away. Immediately
after the king's son woke up, and asked the servant : " Have
they not been here ? " And the man answered : " Yes, they
have been, and say that you can see them again to-morrow,
at this place, but after that they will not return again."
When the unhappy prince heard that, he knew not what to
do with himself, and in his great trouble and misery tore
the hair from his head.

The third day he went down again to the shore, but, fearing
to fall asleep, instead of riding slowly, galloped along the
shore. His servant, however, found an opportunity of
blowing with the bellows behind his neck, and again the
prince fell asleep. A moment after came the nine peahens,
and the eight alighted on the lake and the ninth by him, on
his horse, and sought to awaken him, caressing him. "Arise,
my darling ! Arise, my heart ! Arise, my soul ! " But it
was of no use, he slept on as if dead. Then the peahen said
to the servant : " When your master awakens tell him he
ought to strike off the head of the nail from the lower part,
and then he will find me." Thereupon all the peahens flew
away. Immediately the king's son awoke, and said to his
servant : " Have they been here ? " And the servant answered :
" They have been, and the one which alighted on your horse
103

Serbian ordered me to tell you to strike off the head of the nail from the lower part, and then you will find her." When the prince heard that, he drew his sword and cut off his servant's head.

After that he travelled alone about the world, and after long travelling came to a mountain and remained all night there with a hermit, whom he asked if he knew anything about nine golden peahens. The hermit said : " Eh ! my son, you are lucky ! God has led you in the right place. From this place it is only half a day's walk. But you must go straight on, then you will come to a large gate, which you must pass through ; and, after that, you must keep always to the right hand, and so you will come to the peahens' city, and there find their palace." So next morning the king's son arose, and prepared to go. He thanked the hermit, and went as he had told him. After a while he came to the great gate, and, having passed it, turned to the right, so that at midday he saw the city, and beholding how white it shone, rejoiced very much. When he came into the city he found the palace where lived the nine golden peahens. But at the gate he was stopped by the guard, who demanded who he was, and whence he came. After he had answered these questions, the guards went to announce him to the queen. When the queen heard who he was, she came running out to the gate and took him by the hand to lead him into the palace. She was a young and beautiful maiden, and so there was a great rejoicing when, after a few days, he married her and remained there with her.

One day, some time after their marriage, the queen went out to walk, and the king's son remained in the palace. Before going out, however, the queen gave him the keys of twelve cellars, telling him : " You may go down into all the cellars except the twelfth—that you must on no account open, or it will cost you your head ! She then went away. The king's son whilst remaining in the palace began to

104

wonder what there could be in the twelfth cellar, and soon *Serbian* commenced opening one cellar after the other. When he came to the twelfth he would not at first open it, but again began to wonder very much why he was forbidden to go into it. "What can be in this cellar?" he exclaimed to himself. At last he opened it. In the middle of the cellar lay a big barrel with an open bung-hole, but bound fast round with three iron hoops. Out of the barrel came a voice, saying : "For God's sake, my brother—I am dying with thirst—please give me a cup of water!" Then the king's son took a cup and filled it with water, and emptied it into the barrel. Immediately he had done so one of the hoops burst asunder. Again came the voice from the barrel : "For God's sake, my brother—I am dying of thirst—please give me a cup of water!" The king's son again filled the cup, and took it and emptied it into the barrel, and instantly another hoop burst asunder. The third time the voice came out of the barrel : "For God's sake, my brother—I am dying of thirst—please give me a cup of water!" The king's son again took the cup and filled it, and poured the water into the barrel—and the third hoop burst. Then the barrel fell to pieces, and a dragon flew out of the cellar, and caught the queen on the road and carried her away.

Then the servant who went out with the queen came back quickly, and told the king's son what had happened, and the poor prince knew not what to do with himself, so desperate was he and full of self-reproaches. At length, however, he resolved to set out and travel through the world in search of her. After long journeying, one day he came to a lake and near it, in a little hole, he saw a little fish jumping about. When the fish saw the king's son, she began to beg pitifully : "For God's sake, be my brother, and throw me into the water. Some day I may be of use to you, so take now a little scale from me, and when you need

Serbian me, rub it gently." Then the king's son lifted the little fish from the hole and threw her into the water, after he had taken one small scale, which he wrapped up carefully in a handkerchief. Some time afterwards, as he travelled about the world, he came upon a fox, caught in an iron trap. When the fox saw the prince, he spoke : " In God's name, be a brother to me, and help me to get out of this trap. One day you will need me, so take just one hair from my tail, and when you want me, rub it gently." Then the king's son took a hair from the tail of the fox, and let him free.

Again, as he crossed a mountain, he found a wolf fast in a trap ; and when the wolf saw him, it spoke : " Be a brother to me ; in God's name, set me free, and one day I will help you. Only take a hair from me, and when you need me, rub it gently." So he took a hair, and let the wolf free. After that, the king's son travelled about a very long time, till one day he met a man to whom he said : " For God's sake, brother, have you ever heard any one say where is the palace of the dragon-king ? " The man gave him very particular directions which way to take, and in what length of time he could get there. Then the king's son thanked him, and continued his journey until he came to the city where the dragon lived. When there, he went into the palace, and found therein his wife, and both of them were exceedingly pleased to meet each other, and began to take counsel how they could escape. They resolved to run away, and prepared hastily for the journey. When all was ready they mounted on horseback and galloped away. As soon as they were gone the dragon came home, also on horseback, and, entering his palace, found that the queen had gone away. Then he said to his horse : " What shall we do now ? Shall we eat and drink, or go at once after them ? " The horse answered : " Let us eat and drink first, we shall any-way catch them ; do not be anxious."

106

THE GOLDEN APPLE-TREE

After the dragon had dined, he mounted his horse and *Serbian* in a few moments came up with the runaways. Then he took the queen from the king's son and said to him : " Go now, in God's name ! This time I forgive you because you gave me water in the cellar ; but if your life is dear to you do not come back here any more ! " The unhappy young prince went on his way a little, but could not long resist, so he came back next day to the dragon's palace, and found the queen sitting alone and weeping. Then they began again to consult how they could get away. And the prince said : " When the dragon comes, ask him where he got that horse, and then you will tell me so that I can look for such another one ; perhaps in this way we can escape." He then went away, lest the dragon should come and find him with the queen.

By and by the dragon came home, and the queen began to pet him and speak lovingly to him about many things, till at last she said : " Ah ! what a fine horse you have ! Where did you get such a splendid horse ? " And he answered : " Eh ! where I got it every one cannot get one ! In such and such a mountain lives an old woman who has twelve horses in her stable, and no one can say which is the finest, they are all so beautiful. But in one corner of the stable stands a horse which looks as if he were leprous, but, in truth, he is the very best horse in the whole world. He is the brother of my horse, and whoever gets him may ride to the sky. But whoever wishes to get a horse from that old woman must serve her three days and three nights. She has a mare with a foal, and whoever during three nights guards and keeps for her this mare and this foal has a right to claim the best horse from the old woman's stable. But whoever engages to keep watch over the mare and does not must lose his head ! "

Next day, when the dragon went out, the king's son came, and the queen told him all she had learned from the dragon.

107

Serbian Then the king's son went away to the mountain and found the old woman, and entered her house saying : " God help you, grandmother ! " And she answered : " God help you, too, my son ! What do you wish ? " " I should like to serve you," said the king's son. Then the old woman said : " Well, my son, if you keep my mare safe for three days and three nights I will give you the best horse, and you can choose him yourself ; but if you do not keep the mare safe you shall lose your head."

Then she led him into the courtyard, where all around stakes were ranged. Each of them had on it a man's head, except one stake, which had no head on it, and shouted incessantly : " Oh, grandmother, give me a head ! " The old woman showed all this to the prince, and said : " Look here ! All these were heads of those who tried to keep my mare, and they have lost their heads for their pains ! "

But the prince was not a bit afraid, so he stayed to serve the old woman. When the evening came he mounted the mare and rode her into the field, and the foal followed. He sat still on her back, having made up his mind not to dismount that he might be sure of her. But before midnight he slumbered a little, and when he awoke he found himself sitting on a rail and holding the bridle in his hand. Then he was greatly alarmed, and went instantly to look about to find the mare, and whilst looking for her he came to a piece of water. When he saw the water he remembered the little fish, and took the scale from the handkerchief and rubbed it a little. Then immediately the little fish appeared and said : " What is the matter, my half-brother ? " And he replied : " The mare of the old woman ran away whilst under my charge, and now I do not know where she is ! " And the fish answered : " Here she is, turned to a fish, and the foal to a small one. But strike once upon the water with the bridle and cry out : ' Heigh ! mare of the old
108

THE GOLDEN APPLE-TREE

woman!'" The prince did as he was told, and immediately *Serbian* the mare came, with the foal, out of the water to the shore. Then he put on her the bridle and mounted and rode away to the old woman's house, and the foal followed. When he got there the old woman gave him his breakfast; she, however, took the mare into the stable and beat her with a poker, saying: "Why did you not go down among the fishes, you cursed mare?" And the mare answered: "I have been down to the fishes, but the fish are his friends, and they told him about me." Then the old woman said: "Then go among the foxes!"

When evening came the king's son mounted the mare and rode to the field, and the foal followed the mare. Again he sat on the mare's back until near midnight, when he fell asleep as before. When he awoke, he found himself riding on the rail and holding the bridle in his hand. So he was much frightened, and went to look after the mare. As he went he remembered the words the old woman had said to the mare, and he took from the handkerchief the fox's hair and rubbed it a little between his fingers. All at once the fox stood before him, and asked: "What is the matter, half-brother?" And he said: "The old woman's mare has run away, and I do not know where she can be." Then the fox answered: "Here she is with us; she has turned into a fox, and the foal into a cub; but strike once with the bridle on the earth and cry out: 'Heigh! you old woman's mare!'" So the king's son struck with the bridle on the earth and cried, "Heigh! old woman's mare!" and the mare came and stood, with her foal, near him. He put on the bridle and mounted and rode off home, and the foal followed the mare. When he arrived the old woman gave him his breakfast, and took the mare into the stable and beat her with the poker, crying: "To the foxes, cursed one! To the foxes!" And the mare answered: "I have been with the foxes, but they are his friends, and told him I was there!" Then the

Serbian old woman cried : " If that is so, you must go among the wolves ! "

When it grew dark again the king's son mounted the mare and rode out to the field, and the foal galloped by the side of the mare. Again he sat still on the mare's back until about midnight, when he grew very sleepy and fell into a slumber, as on the former evenings, and when he awoke he found himself riding on the rail, holding the bridle in his hand, just as before. Then, as before, he went in a hurry to look after the mare. As he went he remembered the words the old woman had said to the mare, and took the wolf's hair from the handkerchief and rubbed it a little. Then the wolf came up to him and asked : " What is the matter, half-brother ?." And he answered : " The old woman's mare has run away, and I cannot tell where she is." The wolf said : " Here she is with us ; she has turned herself into a wolf and the foal into a wolf's cub. Strike once with the bridle on the earth and cry out : ' Heigh ! old woman's mare ! ' " And the king's son did so, and instantly the mare came again and stood with the foal beside him. So he bridled her, and galloped home, and the foal followed. When he arrived the old woman gave him his breakfast, but she led the mare into the stable and beat her with the poker, crying : " To the wolves, I said, miserable one ! " Then the mare answered : " I have been to the wolves, but they are his friends, and told him all about me ! " Then the old woman came out of the stable, and the king's son said to her : " Eh ! grandmother, I have served you honestly ; now give me what you promised me." And the old woman answered : " My son, what is promised must be fulfilled. So look here : here are the twelve horses, choose which you like ! " And the prince said : " Why should I be too particular ? Give me only that leprous horse in the corner ! Fine horses are not fitting for me ! But the old woman tried to persuade him to choose another horse, saying : " How

110

can you be so foolish as to choose that leprous thing whilst *Serbian* there are such very fine horses here ? " But he remained firm by his first choice, and said to the old woman : " You ought to give me what I choose, for so you promised." So, when the old woman found she could not make him change his mind, she gave him the scabby horse, and he took leave of her and went away, leading the horse by the halter.

When he came to a forest, he curried and rubbed down the horse, and it shone as bright as gold. He then mounted, and the horse flew as quickly as a bird, and in a few seconds brought him to the dragon's palace. The king's son went in and said to the queen : " Get ready as soon as possible ! " She was soon ready, when they both mounted the horse and began their journey home. Soon after the dragon came home, and when he saw the queen had disappeared, said to his horse : " What shall we do ? Shall we eat and drink first, or shall we pursue them at once ? " The horse answered : " Whether we eat and drink or not it is all one, we shall never reach them."

When the dragon heard that, he got quickly on his horse and galloped after them. When they saw the dragon following them they pushed on quicker, but their horse said : " Do not be afraid ! There is no need to run away." In a very few moments the dragon came very near to them, and his horse said to their horse : " For God's sake, my brother, wait a moment ! I shall kill myself running after you ! " Their horse answered : " Why are you so stupid as to carry that monster ? Fling your heels up and throw him off, and come along with me ! " When the dragon's horse heard that he shook his head angrily and flung his feet high in the air, so that the dragon fell off and brake in pieces, and his horse came up to them. Then the queen mounted him and returned with the king's son happily to her kingdom, where they reigned together in great prosperity until the day of their death.

THE LAST ADVENTURE OF
THYL ULENSPIEGEL

Belgian ULENSPIEGEL and his wife Nele, always young, strong, and beautiful, since love and the spirit of Flanders never grow old, lived peacefully in the Tower of Neere, waiting for the wind of liberty to rise, after so much cruel suffering, and blow upon the land of Belgium.

Ulenspiegel had begged to be appointed commandant and keeper of the Tower, saying that as he had the eyes of an eagle and the ears of a hare, he would be able to see if the Spaniard should attempt to reappear in the liberated provinces, and then he would sound the " wacharm," which in the Flemish tongue means the alarm.

The magistrate granted his request, and for the good service he had done he was given a florin a day, two pints of beer, beans, cheese, biscuit, and three pounds of meat a week.

Thus Ulenspiegel and Nele lived in ease together ; seeing afar with great joy the liberated islands of Zeeland, meadows,

112

woods, castles and fortresses, and the armed vessels of the *Belgian* " Beggars " guarding the coasts.

Often at night they went up on the top of the Tower, and seated on the platform they would talk of fierce battles and happy loves past and yet to be. Hence, they looked down at the sea, which, in the warm summer weather, broke in shining ripples of foam along the shore, throwing them upon the isles like phantoms of fire. And Nele trembled when she saw over the " polders " the will-o'-the-wisps, which are, they say, the souls of the poor dead. And all those places had been battlefields.

These will-o'-the-wisps flitted from the polders, and ran along the dikes : then they returned to the polders, as if loath to leave the bodies from which they had come.

One night Nele said to Ulenspiegel : " See how many of them there are in Dreiveland, and how high they are flying ; I see most over the Isle of Birds. Will you come there with me, Thyl ? We will take the balm that shows things invisible to mortal eyes."

Ulenspiegel replied :

" If it is that balm which made me go to the great Sabbath, I have no more faith in it than in an empty dream."

" You must not deny the power of charms," said Nele.
" Come, Ulenspiegel."

" I will come."

The next day he asked the magistrate for a keen-eyed and faithful veteran to act as his substitute, to guard the Tower and watch over the country.

Then he set out with Nele for the Isle of Birds.

Making their way through fields and by dikes they saw little verdant islets, encircled by the waters of the sea, and on grassy hills that reached as far as the dunes, innumerable plovers and seagulls, which, keeping quite motionless, made as it were white islands with their bodies ; thousands of these birds were flying overhead. The ground was

Belgian studded with nests. Ulenspiegel, bending down to pick up an egg, saw a seagull flying towards him, uttering a cry. At this call, over a hundred came, uttering cries of distress, hovering over the head of Ulenspiegel, and over the neighbouring nests, but not daring to come too close to him.

"Ulenspiegel," said Nele, "these birds are asking us to spare their eggs."

Then, beginning to tremble, she said :

"I am afraid ; the sun is setting, the sky is white, the stars are waking, this is the hour of spirits. See the red vapours that are rising from the ground ! Thyl, my beloved, what monster of hell is opening his fiery jaws thus in the twilight ? Look how the will-o'-the-wisps are dancing over Philipsland, where twice the bloodthirsty king put so many poor creatures to death to satisfy his cruel ambition ; it is at night that the souls of poor men who fell in battle quit the cold Limbo of Purgatory, and come to warm themselves in the mild air of earth ; this is the hour when we may ask anything of Christ, who is the God of good magicians."

"The ashes of Claes lie on my heart," said Ulenspiegel. "Would that Christ could show us those Seven, whose ashes, scattered on the wind, would make Flanders and the whole world happy."

"Man of little faith," said Nele, "the balm will enable you to see them."

"Perhaps," said Ulenspiegel, pointing at Sirius, "if some spirit should come down from that cold star."

Whereupon a will-o'-the-wisp fluttering round him lighted on his finger, and the more he tried to shake it off the closer it clung.

Nele, going to the help of Ulenspiegel, also got a will-o'-the-wisp on her hand.

Then Ulenspiegel, striking at his, said :

"Answer ! Art thou the soul of a 'Beggar' or of a

Spaniard ? If thou art the soul of a ' Beggar,' go to Para- *Belgian*
dise ; if thou art that of a Spaniard, return to the hell
whence thou camest."

Nele said to him :

" Speak not harshly to the souls of the dead, even if they
be the souls of our executioners."

And making her will-o'-the-wisp dance on the tip of her
finger :

" Will-o'-the-wisp," she said, " dear will-o'-the-wisp,
what news do you bring from the land of the spirits ? How
do they busy themselves there ? Do they eat and drink,
seeing they have no mouths ?—for you have none, dear will-
o'-the-wisp. Or do they take human form only when they
enter into the blessed Paradise ? "

" How," said Ulenspiegel, " can you waste your time
talking to that wretched flame which has neither ears to
hear nor mouth to answer you ? "

But Nele, heeding him not, spoke again :

" Will-o'-the-wisp, answer me by dancing, for I will
question thee three times, once in the name of God, once
in the name of the Blessed Virgin, and once in the name of
the elemental spirits, who are the messengers between
God and man."

And this she did, and the will-o'-the-wisp danced three
times.

Then Nele said to Ulenspiegel :

" Take off your clothes, and I will do likewise , here is
the silver box containing the balm of sight. '

" It's all the same to me," said Ulenspiegel.

Then they took off their clothing, anointed their bodies
with the balm of sight, and lay down side by side on the
grass.

The seagulls moaned ; the thunder muttered in clouds
whence flashed the lightning, the moon showed the golden
horns of her crescent but dimly between two clouds ; and

Belgian Ulenspiegel's and Nele's will-o'-the-wisp went off to dance with the rest in the meadow.

Suddenly Nele and her lover were seized by the huge hand of a giant, who tossed them up in the air like children's balls, caught them again, rolled them one upon the other and kneaded them in his hands, threw them into the pools between the hills and pulled them out all covered with seaweed. And as he thus whirled them through space, he sang in a voice that roused all the seagulls in terror :

> " Read, Flea, the mystery !
> Read, Louse, the sacred word
> Which in air, sky, earth
> By seven nails is anchored ! "

And indeed, Ulenspiegel and Nele saw on the grass, in the air, and in the sky, seven tablets of shining brass fastened by seven flaming nails. And on the tablets was written :

> " Sap germinates in dunghills ;
> Seven is bad, but seven is good.
> Diamonds issue out of coal :
> Stupid doctors have wise pupils :
> Seven is bad, but seven is good."

And the giant went along, followed by all the will-o'-the-wisps, chirping like crickets, and saying :

> " Look at him well, he is their great Master,
> Pope of Popes, King of Kings ;
> He takes Cæsar out to graze.
> Look at him well, he's made of wood."

Suddenly his features changed, he seemed thinner, great and mournful. He held a sceptre in one hand and a sword in the other. His name was Pride.

And throwing Nele and Ulenspiegel to the ground, he said :

" I am God."

Then, beside him, mounted on a goat, appeared a ruddy-faced girl, with bare breast, her gown thrown open, her

116

eyes sparkling—her name was Lust ; she was followed by *Belgian* an old Jewess picking up the shells of the seagulls' eggs ; —her name was Avarice ; and a gluttonous monk, gobbling chitterlings, cramming himself with sausages, and gulping incessantly like the sow on which he was mounted—he was Gluttony ; then came Sloth, dragging along, pale and puffy, with lack-lustre eyes, chased by Anger, who drove her with a goad—Sloth wept and lamented, and fell on her knees, overcome with fatigue ; then came lean Envy, with a viper's head and pike's teeth, biting Sloth because it was too leisurely, Anger because it was too lively, Gluttony because it was too replete, Lust because it was too red, Avarice because of the shells, and Pride because of his purple robe and crown. And the will-o'-the-wisps danced around.

And speaking with the plaintive voices of men, women, maidens, and children, they said, moaning :

" Pride, father of ambition, Anger, source of cruelty, ye slew us on the battlefield, in prisons and by torture, to keep your sceptres and your crowns. Envy, thou didst kill the germs of many noble and beautiful thoughts, we are the souls of persecuted inventors ; Avarice, thou didst turn the blood of the poor into gold, we are the spirits of thy victims ; Lust, companion and sister of Murder, the mother of Nero, Messalina, and Philip, King of Spain, thou buyest virtue and rewardest corruption, we are the souls of the dead ; Sloth and Gluttony, ye defile the world and must be swept from it ; we are the souls of the dead.

> " Sap germinates in dunghills ;
> Seven is bad, but seven is good.
> Stupid doctors have wise pupils ;
> How can the vagabond louse contrive
> To have both coal and cinders ? "

And the will-o'-the-wisps said :

" We are fire, the avengers of the ancient tears and pains of the poor ; we take vengeance on the lords who hunted

Belgian human game upon their lands ; we are the avengers of useless battles, of the blood shed in prisons, of men burnt alive, of women and maidens buried alive, the avengers of a past of blood and chains. We are fire, we are the souls of the dead."

At these words the Seven were changed into wooden statues, without losing their original forms.

And a voice said :

" Ulenspiegel, burn this wood."

So Ulenspiegel turned to the will-o'-the-wisps and said : " You who are fire, fulfil your mission."

And the will-o'-the-wisps surrounded the Seven, who were burnt and reduced to ashes. And a river of blood began to flow.

Then from the ashes came forth seven other figures ; the first said :

" I was called Pride, I am now noble Courage." The others spoke in like fashion, and Ulenspiegel and Nele saw Economy rise from Avarice, Vivacity from Anger, Appetite from Gluttony, Emulation from Envy, and from Idleness, the Meditations of poets and philosophers. And Lust, on her goat, was changed into a fair woman whose name was Love.

And the will-o'-the-wisps danced round them joyously.

Ulenspiegel and Nele then heard thousands of gleeful, sonorous voices of hidden men and women, singing to a sound as of castanets :

> " When over earth and sea
> These Seven reign transformed,
> Men, lift up your hands
> For the happiness of the world will have arrived."

And Ulenspiegel said : " The spirits are mocking us."

Then a mighty hand seized Nele by the arm and hurled her into space.

And the spirits sang :

118

LAST ADVENTURE OF THYL ULENSPIEGEL

Belgian

" When the North
Shall kiss the sunset
That will be the end of ruins :
Seek the girdle."

" Oho ! " said Ulenspiegel, " North ? Sunset ? Girdle ?
You talk in riddles, gentle spirits."
Then they sang gleefully :

" North is Holland ;
Belgium is West ;
Girdle is alliance,
Girdle is friendship ! "

" You are wise, gentle spirits," said Ulenspiegel.
Then again they sang gleefully :

" The girdle, poor dear,
Between Holland and Belgium
Will be woven of friendship,
A fair alliance.

Met raedt
En daedt
Met doodt
En bloodt

So would it be,
Were it not for the Scheldt,
Poor dear, were it not for the Scheldt ! "

" Ah ! " said Ulenspiegel, " such is our lamentable lot !
The tears of men and the laughter of Fate ! "

" Alliance of blood
And of death,
Were it not for the Scheldt,"

answered the spirits laughingly.
And a mighty hand seized Ulenspiegel and hurled him
into space.

Belgian   Nele, as she fell to the ground, rubbed her eyes and saw only the sun rising in golden mists, the blades of grass all tipped with gold also, and the sunbeams gilding the plumage of the sleeping seagulls, so that very soon they woke.

Then Nele looked at herself, and seeing she was naked, she dressed herself hastily ; then she saw Ulenspiegel, also naked, and covered him ! Thinking he was asleep, she shook him, but he lay like one dead, and she was seized with fear. " Have I," she said, " killed my beloved with this balm of sight ? I too will die ! Ah ! Thyl, awake ! He is cold as marble ! "

Ulenspiegel did not wake. Two nights and a day passed, and Nele sat and watched her lover in feverish grief.

Now early on the second day, Nele heard the tinkle of a bell, and saw a peasant carrying a spade ; behind him walked, taper in hand, a burgomaster and two sheriffs, the parish priest of Stavenisse and a beadle holding a parasol for him.

They were going, they said, to administer the Sacrament of Extreme Unction to the worthy Jacobsen who had become a " Beggar " from fear, but who when danger was at an end, had returned to die in the bosom of the Holy Roman Church.

Presently they came face to face with the weeping Nele, and saw the body of Ulenspiegel stretched on the grass, covered with his garments. Nele fell on her knees.

" Daughter," said the burgomaster, " what are you doing beside this dead man ? "

Not daring to lift her eyes, she answered :

" I am praying for my beloved, who fell here as if struck by a thunderbolt ; I am alone now, and I would fain die also."

Then the priest rejoiced, saying :

" Ulenspiegel the ' Beggar ' is dead, praise be to God.

Peasant, dig a grave with all speed ; take off his clothes *Belgian* before burying him."

" No," said Nele, rising ; " they shall not be taken off, he would be cold in the earth."

" Dig the grave," said the priest to the peasant who was carrying the spade.

" So be it," said Nele, weeping ; " there are no worms in the sand and lime, and my beloved will remain fair and whole."

And bending over Ulenspiegel's body, she kissed him distractedly with sobs and tears.

The burgomaster, the sheriffs, and the peasants were touched, but the priest ceased not to exclaim joyfully : " The great ' Beggar ' is dead, praise be to God ! "

Then the peasant dug the grave, laid Ulenspiegel in it and covered him with sand.

And the priest said the prayers for the dead over the grave ; all knelt round it ; suddenly there was a great movement under the sand, and Ulenspiegel, sneezing and shaking the sand from his hair, seized the priest by the throat.

" Inquisitor ! " he cried, " you were burying me alive in my sleep ! Where is Nele ? Have you buried her too ? Who are you ? "

The priest cried aloud :

" The great ' Beggar ' has come back to life ! Lord God, receive my soul ! " And he ran like a stag before the hounds.

Nele came to Ulenspiegel :

" Kiss me, beloved," he said.

Then he looked round him again. The two peasants had fled like the priest, throwing spade, chair, and parasol on the ground to run the better ; the burgomaster and the sheriffs, stopping their ears in terror, lay groaning upon the grass.

Belgian Ulenspiegel went to them, and shaking them, he said :
"How can you bury Ulenspiegel, the spirit, Nele, the
heart of Mother Flanders? She too may sleep, but she
cannot die. Come, Nele."

And he went his way with her, singing his sixth song ;
but none know where he sang the last.

THE END